MARCUS L. BOSTON

WHAT IF THIS HAPPENED?

SHORT STORIES
- VOLUME ONE -

UNFAZED PUBLISHING
YOUR MIND IS OUR BUSINESS

TAMPA FLORIDA

ISBN: 9781959275343

LIBRARY OF CONGRESS: 2024938898

This book is a work of fiction. All of these stories, names, characters, places, storylines, backstories, incidents, and outcomes are products of Marcus L. Boston's imagination which are used fictitiously. Any resemblance to actual events, locations, persons living or dead, or any such like, are entirely coincidental.

MARCUS L. BOSTON

UNFAZED PUBLISHING
YOUR MIND IS OUR BUSINESS

WHAT IF THIS HAPPENED?
SHORT STORIES

\-   VOLUME ONE   \-

www.UnfazedPublishing.com

- REVIVIFY -

STORY ONE

*

"... I'm so humbled I was able to speak to you all. Thank you so much. Good night." A strong round of applause accompanied by a standing ovation filled the world famous Chicago Theater. Passionate cheers resonated with the unity we all achieved. I had front row tickets given to me personally by the mayor of Chicago. My husband was my plus one which gave me great joy. Most nights he's busy working in our demanding youth centers across Chicago. We both stood cheering and clapping as the global best selling author waved at us before walking off the stage. We have been waiting on this night for many years. I looked around seeing the theater filled with every culture across the world it seemed. Everyone smiling as we began to exit patiently in orderly fashion. My husband and I walked with our arms intertwined.

We couldn't believe what we both witnessed in our lifetime. We had no small talk on our way home as we held hands in our car. We were speechless and smiled at each other occasionally. We finally heard Daquan Jackson in person.

Mr. Jackson was the first voice of reason who rose from the embers of our shame. He was the doctor and nurse to our wounded spirits. Daquan provided structure and comfort in the midst of being stripped of all dignity and integrity. These words were like a desert in the black community. Our existence accurately felt less than human. His terms and expressions resuscitated something in our black culture which has been long since forgotten. You'll understand soon.

After we arrived at our beautiful home in the Englewood area in Chicago, my husband played some soft jazz as we both prepared for bed. Our neighborhood looks a lot like the audience we saw earlier this evening. It used to be depleted and full of violence. After I finished freshing up, I wore his favorite pajamas he loved to see me in. I found him waiting for me on our very silky love seat. I sat in his lap comfortably. I've always loved his embrace and he's always demonstrated his affection towards me. We held each other as the smooth jazz added more comfort and ease with our in awe dispostions from seeing Daquan Jackson. Seeing him had the same effect when all black people became unified. We thought we would never see this day. Martin Luther King Jr. would have cried tears of joy along with Malcom X. Who would have thought in one hundred years a real change would take place in the black community. There was no political leader who took the forefront leading us to this place; that's the crazy part about how it happened. Oh, by the way, my name is Grace. My husband's name is James Clark, and I love being Mrs. Grace Clark.

On July 4th, 2029, the black community changed forever. Chicago gangs organized and went to L.A.. We witnessed it live on social media and on many television networks. All eyes were on L.A. as their streets became a warzone. The black gangs of L.A. didn't know this was coming. No one really knew what happened except the Chicago gangs. Lots of black men died that day and plenty of black women. As this gangwar was taking place live, many Chicago residents started watching it. Various fathers, mothers, and siblings saw their family members shooting and killing in real time. These family members stopped their cookouts and began packing. Fear gripped them because they knew how their son/brother/cousin/nephew/uncle lived their life. It was bad enough they were killing black people in Chicago, but now they went to L.A. to kill more black people. It was almost as if these families planned to move together. Those who owned trucks took everything and told no one where they were going. Those who had less resources only took their clothes and keepsakes. Without saying a word to each other, everyone knew L.A. gangs were coming to Chicago in retaliation. In Chicago, on that day, not one person was shot or killed.

L.A. gangs were caught off guard and suffered great losses. With there being no unity or truces among the L. A. gangs, many of them assumed it was local gangs targeting them. Those who could make calls and gather their soldiers, attacked their known enemies which aided Chicago. It appeared Chicago gangs were aware this would happen as they arrived on the scene of active shootings between L. A. gangs. Both L. A. gangs were obliterated as they shot at each other and mutually received slugs from Chicago gangs. The looks on the L.A. gangs faces prior to death spoke volumes. There was so much confusion some gang members lowered their weapons as they looked around stunned. Many hard exteriors of masculinity became countenances of terror. Some of them broke down in tears seconds before receiving multiple shots. Tears were still running down their faces as they exhaled for the last time. We witnessed this on a gang members live feed. Little did he know he was going to capture his last breath to the world.

Cookouts and bbqs were massacres. It was as if the gangs of Chicago knew every place L.A. gangmembers families would be. Every family of

L.A. gangs suffered casualties; some greater than others. Too much innocent blood was shed. Grandparents, parents, and grandchildren were killed without mercy. Entire generations were wiped out at the same time. Some L.A. gang members played dead at one cookout and overheard someone say, "Jobs done. Let's get back to Chicago." L.A. Police tried to intervene, but after 14 police were killed, they retreated and watched it play out with us. Police called in favors to find out what weapons were being used in this tragedy. Law enforcement couldn't believe how well organized this attack was as they watched it play out. The police noticed there was no gang activity from non black gangs during the 4th of July. Everyone involved was black.

Once the gangs of Chicago completed their offensive onslaught, they even had an exit plan out of L.A.. It was like a movie scene as police helicopers and police cars lost evading individuals. L.A. Police knew Chicago had great assistance to execute escaping L.A.. Their weapons destroyed 2 helicopers and 3 police cars. After the police within those vehicles were pronounced dead at their locations, they stopped all pursuing vehicles. The L.A. Police death toll was now 24. 14 were black.

In the aftermath of this gangwar, the L.A. Police ran finger prints of those who were found dead. Most were from local gangs, but police national records indicated some were from Chicago. L.A. Police contacted the Chicago Police Department (CPD) and shared their findings. CPD were astounded! This information was relayed to the chain of command at CPD, and personally delivered to the mayor Chicago. They knew this was a very bad situation. The mayor didn't want to deal with this. "What do we do?" The mayor Chicago asked the police officers in his home. No one had answers. The fear of L.A. gangs coming to Chicago was written in their demeanor. "How do we prepare the city of Chicago? What if they come with the same weapons or worse?" The mayor added with no one answering again. "What's the..." The mayor stopped understanding the weight and pressure wrapping around him. He needed some air. As he opened the front door of his secured home, he was scared to walk out. Suddenly, his mobile phone sounded jarring everyone. It was the President of the United States (Potus). "Mr. President thank you for the call...." "...I'll get right to the point. Prepare your national guard now. I'm sending weapons to help you protect Chicago. It's been brought to my attention the weapons used in L.A. are our new weapons. We haven't used them in the field as of yet. We're working to find out who is behind this. Your national guard will be given proper gear to protect them against these weapons. You're not alone. I'm sure you're concerned you'll be blamed for this. Well, those weapons will cause me to be at fault not you. I'll be in touch." Potus words gave the mayor of Chicago some comfort knowing he wasn't alone and assistance was coming. He immediately called to have the Illinois National Guard prepped and readied, but he was certainly worried Chicago would experience what happened in L.A..

When the final number of black men killed was released to the public, it echoed across the globe. Six thousand nine hundred ninety seven black men were dead. The bloodshed lasted around ten hours. It was so strategic. The assault began at two oclock in the afternoon and ended around midnight. Forty two gang members from Chicago were killed. Words cannot describe the jolt the black community felt. The online live videos, traffic cameras, business cameras, security cameras, and other recordings, were all gathered together by the police. Warrants were created for those identifed by Chicago Police. Of the almost seven thousand dead, about half were non gang members. Grandfathers, fathers who were gang members, and their sons. The total number of black women and black girls dead was not released to the public. There weren't enough local detectives to gather information from all the crime scenes. Backyards, parks, and beaches were filled with bodies of the dead. The only non-blacks killed were at the beaches. No one knew how the Chicago gangs pulled this off. This was a great mystery.

What was left of the L.A. gangs wasn't enough to retaliate against Chicago. So many of those who survived were broken by the deaths of their families; especially those who witnessed it right in front of them. A few hundred lived long enough to tell their families they loved them, and died in the hospital. Some confessed to crimes they were guilty of prior to dying after talking to a Chaplain. The families who had surviving members were afraid Chicago gangs would come back. The grieving families needed answers, but some already knew what happened. When L.A. police talked to them, they didn't say anything. Their guilty body language was evident. "What information are they withholding?" One L.A. Police officer asked out loud. All faces turned toward him. He abruptly blurted out these words as he walked off, "Well, if you don't want justice for your family, why should I?" No one uttered a word as the police left the hospital. A few gang members were in a coma for several weeks. No police bothered to visit. They didn't want to waste their time speaking to families who acted as if they were mute.

Meanwhile in Chicago, as the gangs returned, they found they had no homes or families. Houses and apartments were abandoned. They called their families and couldn't get a hold of no one. These people disappearred without a trace. They even quit their jobs. Friends of their families also disappearred and changed their phone numbers. It was almost as if this was planned years in advance. As gang members communicated and discovered all of their families were gone, they understood what took place. They began planning for L.A. to come to Chicago. Every black neighborhood in Chicago was quiet. No children played outside. As Labor Day approached, local news sources all reported food sales were down. There would be no cookouts this Labor Day Weekend.

The Chicago Police Department took into custody as many gang members who were connected to those seen on video as they could find. None of them cooperated with the police. No one snitched. The gang members who were identified on L.A. videos couldn't be found. They were in hiding. Public transit was also quiet. Everything about the city of Chicago was changed almost in an instant. No one knew how the gangs of Chicago formed a peace treaty. It was rumored that L.A. gangs called Chicago gangs weak and obsolete. It was also rumored these things were said on social media, but no such videos were ever found. What really happened?

Back in L.A., the dead bodies were starting to decompose because the crime scenes were openly exposed to the warm California weather. Detectives from other cities and states volunteered to assist with the open investigations. Most people just wanted these bodies off the streets. However, investagations were needed. The findings at every crime scene was evidence of weapons no one could identify. Some black people were angry over these investigations. They were blaming the L.A. Police of not caring because they were black dead bodies. These angry black voices were very few in number.

Black people were too sad and stung to find fault outside of ourselves. The images of these warzones featuring black versus black shut the mouths of many black people across the nation.

There was something different about this situation. The black activists disappearred. The few angry pro black voices also disappearred. No black people talked about this on television networks. Most black podcasters were silent except for a few and they were heavily criticized until they were cancelled. Even though their podcast videos didn't even go viral, they were still cancelled. Black people didn't want to hear anything adding more attention to this massacre. The aerial views of black dead bodies in backyards and parks was too much for our black community. The images of children, women, and the elderly laying dead, was severely crushing to obeserve. Bodies littered our neighborhoods. No black person admitted this openly, but this broke the back of all African Americans.

White supremacists came forward in the

aftermath of this dark event. Instead of black people being outraged at the very sight of them, we did something on the contrary which was very different for us. We actually listened to everything they had to say. Some of them took credit as if they orchestrated this as a terrorist attack. Some laughed profoundly with new suggestions of how they will celebrate the fourth of July more because of this wonderful historical event. The lowest blow came when **KKK** grand wizard acutely expressed these words as he addressed their following, "What a fourth of July!" The crowd exploded with roaring cheers which brought tears to my eyes. "My fellow white people. Does it get any better than this?" This was a private clan rally which was leaked on purpose. No hoods. Their faces..., I will never forget their faces. Pleasure. Joy. Sincere appreciation for the dead black bodies displayed for the world to see. "My fellow Klansmen. It's with unlimited happiness that I demonstrate the heart of all of us present." There was a curtain to the side of his platform. It opened. There was an open coffin with a sign that read, "6997 Black Dead Bodies." Above the coffin was a plaque with engraving I will never utter. "It's been 8 days and the stench, no, the sweet stench of black rotten flesh is in the air of L.A. This aroma will forever be captured, treasured, by all of us forever. Why is this coffin here? Well, we are going to do what many nigger families can't do at this time. We are going to bury their bodies today." The sound which erupted actually felt like a nail to the coffin. It felt like a real funeral. This video went viral, and there we were as black people watching it. Not one of us expressed anger. We sat in silence as noiseless tears fell from our eyes. "This sign represents all of the niggers who killed each other." He placed the sign into the coffin. "Goodbye niggers. Thanks for murdering each other. Keep up the great work." Shouts of satisfaction reverberated as they watched him pour gasoline onto the coffin. "Ashes to ashes. Dust to dust. Thank you niggers. Keep killing for us." He closed the coffin with the sign inside and poured more gasoline on it. "Don't you just love this? I'm so happy I lived to see this day. I thought I hated niggers. Not anymore." Boos begin to sound, but quieted when he lifted his hands. "I love niggers who kill niggers! They hate each other more than we hate them!" He started laughing, "... Yep, I love watching ghetto gangster movies. I love watching niggers kill each other. It's a blessing from God. It's better than lynching although I love me a good lynching. Yep, I love me a good lynching. Almost 7,000 niggers died in one day. Maybe next time we can get 10,000 dead niggers!" Electric cheers exploded from the crowd as our tears increased. "I have the live footage saved on my phone. I'll be watching this for the rest of my life and hoping these dumb stupid niggers do it again. **CHICAGO IS MY KIND OF TOWN!!! NOW LIGHT THAT MOTHERFUCKING COFFIN UP!!!**"

As the coffin burned they celebrated. It was a party rejoicing the death of 7,000 blacks. The faces of these **KKK** members were etched in the minds of many black people. We were appalled at some of the white faces we recognized. His final remarks destroyed what was left of the dignity and intrigrity carried by the most honorable people in our black community. He raised his hands and everyone quieted down, "Are we ready?" He looked at someone and they gave him a thumbs up. A screen projection began showing a film. This film starcased the dead bodies while they played a very ratchet trap rap song. The video was edited to feature black women twerking over the dead bodies. This video looked very real. Maybe AI created it. They also featured videos of black women twerking at funerals and on top of coffins. This combination mixed with actual footage with trap, furthered our embarrassment as black people. When the video ended, a detonation of applause boomed as the **KKK** members slapped high 5s as some danced "trap rap" dances mocking us.

The trap song continued as he pointed to the burning coffin. By this time the fires were dying down. While the music played, the coffin began to descend into the ground. The applause continued as several white men walked over to the coffin. Out of nowhere a dumptruck backed up toward the coffin. The white men signaled the dumptruck which released dirt on top of the coffin. It's like my heart stopped as I watched the white men take shovels to completely bury the coffin. They even added a headstone. "7000 Dead Niggers July 4th, 2029." Many blacks watching this video had mental breaks, while some had outbursts, wailing, and screams. We were holistically annihilated as a community. "Nothing like nigger hoes twerking over dead niggers. Let's always cherish this event. Niggers killing niggers is always a pleasure..." I never saw the rest of it. My husband viewed the entire video. I've never seen him cry and sob so deeply. The black community was never the same, but something good would take place. We just didn't know it yet.

We were stagnant for many years once we started killing each other in the late 80s and early 90s. Twerking became a pandemic of its own. Once twerking started, it never stopped until it dominated all cultures in the United States. There were no more classy sophisticated music award shows. Everything involving black people became ratchet, filthy, immoral, and plain debaucherous. We couldn't stop it although we tried. Anything we said to teach younger blacks a better way was considered hating on them. No one listened to us. Our voices went unheard for many years. Some of us gave up. We stopped trying to teach once we recognized our characters were rejected. However, all of this changed once this happened.

A few live videos of the massacre displayed black women twerking at cookouts and bbqs just before gun shots ended their lives. These guns had no sound. The looks on their faces as their loved ones fell down bleeding..., smh. No one knew what was happening. Normally they could hear where the shots were coming from and run away. In this case, they were twerking and out of the blue they were shot. It was worse than a horror movie. I have never understood the black people who loved the sound of gun fire. Why? Moreover, they seemed happy while they ran for safety. What was fun about this? I've never understood it. Nonetheless, those who lived had a very strong sobering epiphany. For some, their baby daddy died, and for others, all of their baby daddies died. Many lost their children. Twerking was never viewed the same way after the KKK video and these videos of women dying while twerking.

Every section, every area, every category, and every level of African American life in the United States was affected. Black Hollywood was changed forever. African American stars were put on the spot with various questions. They had no comments. Some of them were pressed until they reacted with anger. Some cried as they hurried away from the cameras and questions. Many black stars withdrew from film productions that featured them as gang members, drug dealers, hoes, strippers, and twerkers. Black film producers canceled all gangster films. Everything changed.

I can't speak for other black families, but my black family decided to talk about it. This talk, well, discussion, was filled with compassion and sorrow.

There was no anger, this time. There was no one blaming anyone, this time. We cried together. Our talk was not about a solution. We all opened our hearts sharing our personal feelings. Not one of us had any solutions. As I talked with more black people, I found out many families came together like ours. No one had a solution. This time, no one had anything to say like, "We have to stop black on black crime." Wasn't said. "We must love each other and stop killing each other." Wasn't said. No one said anything. Well, other nationalities expressed their feelings, but we weren't listening. Those videos went viral, but not because black people were watching them. There was an unspoken unity which was taking place that none of us were aware of. It was very similar to the unspoken unity during the Montgomery Alabama Riverboat Fight August 5th, 2023. We rejoiced to see each other coming to aid a brother getting beat up by white people. This situation, on the other hand, ignited something we didn't recognize. Our shame, and disappointment, in what we witnessed changed us. As the weeks passed by, we saw it unfold little by little.

The things which caused major separations between us were being pulled apart by our conversations in our families. Strong independent black women dropped their title. The number of marriages dwindled in the United States because of the podcast wars between black men and black women. The Passport Bros movement came to an end with black men. There was something in the hearts of black men that destroyed the desire for other nationalities of women after this July 4th. Many of these black men lost love ones and flew back to the United States to support their families. Black men strongly desired to take the lead in finding solutions for our community. This is when Mr. Daquan Jackson released his book, "REVIVIFY! The New Vision & Direction For Our Community." His handsome face was on the cover. Black men read this book and recommended it to their families. Within months it was a best seller.

Sobriety took over our community. As we

continued talking with our families, it made it easier to talk with other black families. We talked with our friends families, and through many deep compassionate talks, coupled with the information in Daquan's book, the solutions began to come to the forefront. Black families knew what they had to do and honestly, we always knew what needed to be done. Mr. Jackson expressed this boldly in his book. However, no one desired to do what was always needed to be done. Mothers and fathers snitched on their children. Grandparents, uncles, cousins, nephews, sisters, and other relatives, all began to inform the police who the gang members were on the videos. It didn't stop there. Every black neighborhood began to inform police of crimes they witnessed. Murders started being solved in record numbers. Police were beyond surprised. Many individuals were guilty of many murders in their own neighborhood. Some had very high numbers. There were some black people who tried to fight against this truth movement and tried to intimidate their family members into shutting their mouths, but the entire family came together against them. Black gangs were dismantled and ended during this season. Every crime witnessed was reported immediately. All black people who didn't want to comply had to change their lives. Once they knew witnesses will come forth regardless of threats, it was over. Communities came together to protect each other from retaliation and backlash from criminals out on bail. Most families stopped bailing out their family members they believed were guilty. Entire families and neighborhoods armed themselves, took gun classes, received gun licenses, and went to gun ranges. The elderly who used to be easy victims found themselves using their weapons they were trained to use. It was unbelievable how black communities came together. The police started trusting the black community and the fear of being killed by black people departed.

Black stars began after school programs and opened different businesses in black neighborhoods to help us heal. No one had to ask for money and black stars freely gave in abundance. Furthermore, black programs for the homeless and needy also opened. We started taking care of each other instead of criticizing the lives of those who were struggling. The black people who dared to go against the grain of this movement were canceled. Rappers who dared to have lyrics of killing and female rappers with ratchet lyrics were all canceled by the black community. Record companies were losing money. Nonblacks who became accustomed to using "nigger" had to change. Why? Black people came together to stop using the word altogether. Black people who were reluctant to join us quickly learned, "It was all aboard or nothing."

Daquan Jackson's book was now an international best seller. He identified all of these things with a caring heart. He travelled to different black communities and documented what was taking place. He compared his findings and discovered many of the same things were taking place in black communities everywhere. The most impressive statistic was gun violence dropped 97 percent after July 4th. Within a years time, there was no gun violence of any kind in most black neighborhoods. All crimes were reported and the term "snitch" was canceled. Daquan Jackson's book helped every black community to become unified. The world watched us in disbelief. Many said it wouldn't last, but here we are twenty five years later. Safe black neighborhoods, education is valuable again, and the black community regained integrity, dignity, and honor. Young black men walked away from selling drugs. Some of them were killed by the drug cartels they worked for, but witnesses came forth and arrests were made. Black families stock piled guns. Trying to recruit new drug dealers was almost impossible. With all of the neighborhood programs, those who were in need received helped and didn't have to resort to selling drugs. Nonetheless, although some kept trying to sell drugs, the drug user population dwendled. We had programs to help individuals break their drug habits. Prostitution also dwindled. As integrity, dignity, and honor was rebuilt in the black community, this became the driving force for many black people to become polititians. The solutions we had for our black neighborhoods became the solutions for nonblack neighborhoods. Lots of black people returned to the church. It was an amazing transition and many churches opened their facilities for many programs to be established. Those who already had such programs, received funds to expand to assist more people. Daquan Jackson's book captured us and he documented our rise from the July 4th tragedy. Although Daquan takes no credit, it was his book that went global with solutions to recover from 6997. Someone finally released the number of black women and children who died that day, 1003. 8000 thousand black people died July 4th. A pastor had a sermon entitled, "Eight Thousand Reasons To Change." This message went viral on all social media. He passionately stated, "It took eight thousand deaths for Daquan Jackson to write his book. Eight... is the number... of 'new beginnings.' From this tragedy... came the remedy." Those of us who didn't know the number "8" is the number of new beginnings, cried when this pastor explained their revelation.

Maybe I'll write a book about the things my husband and I did in our communities here in Chicago. I'm so happy now. Not just because of my own individual success. I'm happy because we as a community are finally loving each other and proud to be black. At our darkest moment, we took unified action which helped us achieve what seemed impossible. Martin Luther King's dream is now a reality and I personally wish he could have lived to see this day manifest. He said I may not get there with you. How I wish... well, you already know. Oh yeah, the mayor of Chicago; let's just say he and Potus were in the hot seat until they actually found the guilty parties. It turned out to be multiple men and women from various parts of the military branches. Some of these people were involved in Chicago gangs before joining the military. The black community didn't care who was at fault anymore. We focused on the end result and didn't follow the politics involved. Arrests were made though, ...and they pleaded guilty. We were satisfied they took accountability. At least they confessed and explained how they caused a truce with Chicago gangs. The military trained them and prepared them to attack L.A. black gangs. The nonblack gangs were notified and their entire families took 4th of July vacations outside of L.A.. We really had no words during this phase which took two years. We were busy rebuilding our dignity and integrity. If only Martin Luther King could have witnessed our unification. I say this repeatedly because he gave his life trying to get us where we are presently. Well, thanks for listening to my story. I pray you all have a wonderful evening. God bless." Mrs. Grace Clark received a standing ovation...

- INCREDULITY -

STORY TWO

* *

[GOD'S SERVANT] LIVE 7 watching

[COMMENTS]

... Look at him! He's a fucking idiot!

I couldn't have said it better. Why are we watching this guy?

Because he's entertaining! CTFU!

Every week we are on this dumb ass live. This is my last one. I'm done.

I'm with you. Let's get the fuck off of here!

LIVE 2 watching

"... God is real. He really sent His son to die for our sins. We are living in the last days..."

[COMMENTS]

SHUT THE FUCK UP! JESUS AIN'T COMING! HOW LONG WILL Y'ALL KEEP LYING TO US! IF JESUS IS REAL, WHY IS THE WORLD SO BAD? WHY AM I HERE?

WHAT THE FUCK IS WRONG WITH ME?

LIVE 1 watching

"... The world is bad because of sin. The world is bad because of man's sin natures and man keeps choosing to do things that harm our fellow humans. It's not God's fault the world is bad..."

[COMMENTS]

Sir. I don't want to be mean or disrespectful to you. I hear you like I heard my grandmother, but I watched her die an agonizing death. If Jesus is real, why didn't He heal her?

LIVE 1 watching

"... I'm very sorry to hear about your grandmother. I'm sure if I knew more information, maybe I could discern what happened. Bad things happen to Christians. You see it in the bible and in the world today..."

[COMMENTS]

I don't care about the world or what happened in the bible. I cared about my grandmother. Why didn't Jesus heal her? She said Jesus is real, but I didn't see Jesus heal her. Your bible says Jesus is a healer. Right...?

LIVE 1 watching

"... Right. The bible says Jesus is a healer."

[COMMENTS]

I just don't believe it. My grandmother prayed and had devotion every day, and she died with multiple diseases and she became disabled. That didn't stop her. She believed Jesus could heal her, but He didn't. I will not becoming back to your LIVE ever again. I want to believe, but I don't want to believe in something that isn't real. Take care.

LIVE 0 watching

"..........................." Live Ended.

The person streaming this social media live broadcast is a no named man of God. He is not anywhere close to being in the limelight. He doesn't have a big following. The few who did watch him ridiculed and insulted him on purpose. He never gave his name on his streams. He only called himself, "God's Servant." He would say many times He represents God and desires to be His voice. He never took an offering or asked anyone for a single donation. This guy never talked about himself. I know this because I was on his live faithfully trying to believe what he was saying about the bible, but my grandmother, well.... The next live he had I did not watch while he was live. I watched the replay. I couldn't believe what I witnessed. I actually heard him out for the entire broadcast. I'll just let you listen to it for yourself. [GOD'S SERVANT] was Live.

[0 SHARE(S)]

"Welcome to the God's Servant Podcast. To God be the glory both now and forever. This morning I want to acknowledge a comment I received yesterday. A viewer shared their grandmother believed Jesus would heal her, but He didn't. This viewer said she died a very painful death, but she was faithful. Well, I'm faithful too. My life isn't the best life. I know I don't talk about myself, but today I'll share some of my life. Many people in my own family died horrible deaths, but they believed in Jesus. At least they are with Jesus now and for all eternity. I have a minimum wage job. I attend a small store front church which does not have enough resources to help us as members of this church. The pastor works a job, and so do the others in the church leadership. We love Jesus. We are not the big time examples you see with mega ministries, nice clothes, and nice cars. As a matter of fact, I don't have a car. I ride a bike and if I'm late I'll take a bus. After reading those comments yesterday I've come to this conclusion. Maybe Jesus isn't real. Christians say I should be living a life more abundantly. They teach I should be prosperous and I'm not. I have many unanswered prayers, but I keep going. I've never seen Jesus or had an encounter with angels. All I have is my faith and now I may not have that anymore. I admit I am in doubt right now. Maybe I'm now like Thomas who needed to see proof about Jesus. All I do is promote Jesus and I do not see miracles, but I believe; well, I did. This will be my last broadcast. I've been humiliated too many times on this Live and I've never said anything. I really believed in walking in love and forgiveness. I am abstinent and I've been yielding my life to Jesus for years. I'm always pursuing to be a better Christian. Even now my personal name is not important. I'm thinking of deleting this profile. No one is listening to me. I'm not making a difference in anyone's life. So, I'm done with this..."

Tears began forming in his eyes. He tried to hold it together, but soon thereafter he wept.

[GOD'S SERVANT] was Live.

[0 SHARE(S)]

"... I'm so tired... I just can't believe how my life is... (Crying very hard.) I guess you're not real Jesus.... I've asked for so many things, and nothing has happened... Yet, I kept doing what I believe you wanted me to do... (His eyes are turning dark red.) I just don't understand anything about you and how you do things. Why can't you do miracles for me? Why not show the whole world that you are real Jesus? Why not shut everyone's mouth who's talking against you? (He's now crying uncontrollably.) ... Why not?... Huh?.....................
Is that too much to ask? .... Why not??

You're God!!!!!!!!!!! Show us you're God!!!!!!!"

All of a sudden, he was real quiet and his eyes were stretched wide open. When his mouth dropped and stayed open, I knew something was happening. I felt peace as I watched this broadcast. I also started feeling warm all over. Everything felt like a pond that didn't have any wind blowing over it. I stared at him in this amazing feeling. He rose out of his chair and went to his knees. As soon as his knees hit the floor he went face forward to the floor. He sobbed,

[GOD'S SERVANT] was Live.

[0 SHARE(S)]

"Yes Lord.   Yes Lord.   Yes Lord.

Yes Lord.   Yes Lord."

He looked and sounded as if he was responding to someone. I wondered was God speaking to him. I was so curious because of this wondering feeling of peace and calm I had as I watched him on his face flat on the floor. I'm glad he sat on a sofa during his broadcast with his camera or phone set up several feet in front of him. Out on nowhere he cried saying hallelujah. I don't know why, but I started crying with him. I didn't hear anything or see anything, but I felt like I was loved so deeply. I couldn't resist or fight this strong feeling of love. I knew this was God and I cried in a way almost identical to him. As I cried I wished I knew his name. I wasn't ready when he rolled over and slowly eased himself back onto his sofa. He began to say,

[GOD'S SERVANT] was Live.

[0 SHARE(S)]

"...This is my first ever encounter with God. I have never felt His love upon me. He reassurred me He is real and He will do something for me to prove Himself to the world. God said to me, 'I will do a thing never ever done on earth to prove myself to my unbelieving children. Yet, I will not show myself or speak so the entire world hears me. For 40 days and 40 nights I will heal everyone across the globe of every illness, every disease, and every disability. I do not this thing to prove my power, but I do this thing for you. You will witness unbelief across this world which will astonish you. Yet, I already see it. At the end of these 40 days and 40 nights, my unbelieving children will still not believe I did this amazing thing. Remember I said blessed are they that believe who have not seen. All hospitals and nursing homes will be empty. Your pharmaceutical companys will suffer great loss over these days, but they will recover their losses. The blind shall see. The deaf shall hear. Anyone who dies an hour before noon tomorrow central standard time, I will raise from the dead. Once these days are completed they shall die at the same time I raised them from the dead. No one will die over these 40 days and 40 nights. Yet, my unbelieving children will not believe this wonderful thing is because of me. I want you to warn the world of these things. Whatever illness or disease they had will return once these days are completed. Warn them to return to the place where they were so they will not be in the wrong place as their bodies return to it's previous condition. Says the Lord your God.'"

If you're looking at this replay, please share this broadcast. Share it with everyone you know. The 40 days and 40 nights begins tomorrow worldwide at noon central standard time. Please help me spread the word. God bless you and thank you in advance for sharing."

[COMMENTS]

I watched the replay and I shared it to all my social media. God bless you.

[1 SHARE(S)]

After I shared this broadcast I relaxed in silence. Even though I know what I felt, I found it extremely hard to believe everyone in the world will be healed of their diseases. What if God does it? Surely if this happens everyone would know it's God, right? Of course, they would know it's God. There is no way everyone would have unbelief. I laid in bed thinking about this for hours. I received a few replies from my family and friends about my share. They laughed at me. All I said was, "If it happens you know God did it." The laughter stopped. After responding to the last text message, I decided to go on my own social media platforms live. I kept it real quick and straight to the point. I repeated what God's servant stated and added, "What if this happens? Will you believe in God if this happens?" I normally had plenty of people commenting, but during this broadcast, I didn't have any comments at all. I blamed this on the fact it was very late, but I still had several hundred people who watched my live. Wow, no one said anything? Interesting. Anyway, I made sure I shared what the no named preacher declared. I wondered if this would happen and if it did happen, how amazing would this thing be?

I couldn't sleep and wondered if the no named preacher could sleep. I was still up when I saw the break of day. There I was in great anticipation of what might happen today. I showered and prepared for my day at work. I commuted on public transit, and quickly regretted it because we had some major delays. I called my job informing them I would be late. Fortunately for me, I had to be at work at 11am. However, this really bothered me being late. I should have been to work a full hour before I had to begin. Instead, I'm stuck on the train in the subway. I had my AirPods on and didn't bother listening to the announcment explaining the delay. I noticed several passengers displayed their anger and disgust because our train was standing still. I didn't realize we were standing over 45 minutes. I removed my AirPods to hear the conversations of these passengers. After a minute I placed my AirPods back on. It was the same angry talk I've heard a million times before. Once our train began moving, there was a round of applause which filled our rail car. I decided to get off although it wasn't my station stop. I just needed some fresh air. With everything going on I forgot about the no named preacher and what could possibly happen at noon today. I called my job again when "BOOM!" A tired blew out on a semi-truck flying off the axle. "Splack!" The tire hit two people walking on the side walk. They were both hit in the head and were on the side walk bleeding. I told my job I needed to call 911. The 911 operator sent assistance, but it was too late. The man and woman died seconds apart from their head injuries. When medical assistance arrived, they worked on both individuals, but were unsuccessful. I was asked if I witnessed what happened and shared in detail what I observed. While we were yet talking, we all heard a screech which made us turn our heads simultaneously. A car ran a redlight hitting a man causing him to be airborne. The man was immediately hit by a passing bus with the green light dying instantly. The car running the redlight was hit by the car the bus just passed. The front end of the car was damaged as it hit the drivers side front door. The driver of the car who ran the redlight had minor injuries and was visibly shook up because they hit someone. The driver claimed they dropped their coffee and hit the gas by accident.

This intersection was now at a complete stand still. Another ambulance arrived and was updated by the other medical staff on the scene. This was so sad and I couldn't believe I witnessed all of this. A news van arrived and started interviewing bystanders. I was happy they didn't talk to me. I called my job back who already knew what was taking place because they were watching me live on the news. My supervisor suggested, "Why don't you go home and relax? It's almost noon. Take this day and unwind from what you experienced today." I was confounded when I responded, "Huh? What time is it?" "Mike, it's 11:59am." All of a sudden with excitement I informed my supervisor, "Ok. Mr. Webb. We might witness some miracles today. As a matter of fact in one minute..." "Mike, Mike..., calm down. What are you talking about?..." "...Just keep watching the news live. I'll explain it later. I got to go."

I went live on all of my social media just as the time changed to 12:00pm. There were 3 bodies covered with white sheets. My heart started pounding and I was actually hoping the miraculous took place, but nothing happened. By 12:05pm, I ceased my live video. I was soooo disappointed. I couldn't believe I was actually hoping this happened. I guess I really wanted God to be real. I guess He's not real. I decided to go to work anyway. The area was now considered a crime scene by police. The semi-truck company was supposed to get new wheels for their entire fleet, but failed to do so. In addition, the driver who ran the redlight was arrested for vehicular homicide. The bus driver was not found at fault. The police questioned many of us and took our information. I stood around for several minutes and left the scene around 12:40pm.

I arrived at work at 12:57pm and Mr. Webb wasted no time approaching me, "I thought I told you to go home? You are no good to us if you're not focused on the project we are working on. I need you totally here mentally. Hello? Are you listening to me Mike?... Hello..." "... Ah yes, ...I'm listening to you. I'm just disappointed..." "... Disappointed at what? Coming to work? Not being focused on our project? Mike, like I said, go home..." "EVERYONE! COME TO THE TV!!! OMG!!! LOOK!!!" Mr. Webb, Mike, and everyone in the office ran together to see what was on the television. News Reporter Joanne, "... We are still in disbelief at what has taken place. Maybe there is a rational explaination for all of this." News anchor David, "Joanne, these people were prononuced dead about an hour ago. I trust our ambulance workers know what a pulse and heartbeat is. We saw one of them sit up while they were covered in their white sheet as you talked. Let's call this what it really is. It's a mirale." "Now David, let's not get ahead of ourselves here..."

Mike's jaw was dropped the entire time watching the live news. He explained everything to Mr. Webb and all of his coworkers. As they stood there watching the news. More new reports started coming in from other news reporters of miracles taking place. As Mike watched the news, tears fell from his eyes. He said it very softly and everyone heard him, "God is real." No one fought against Mike. No one challenged him. There were no words for all of the miracles taken place. As they continued watching the news, international news reports started coming in. Mike cried deeply and suddenly thought to go to the no named preachers podcast to see if he was Live.

[GOD'S SERVANT] LIVE 1 watching

[0 COMMENTS]

As I tuned into God's Servant Podcast, he was praising God and instantly knew I was the only one watching. I logged out and continued watching the news with my office family. The news broadcast was as it was the day Michael Jackson died. Every channel covered the miracles taking place all over the world. There were too many to count. As the hours passed by we didn't get any work completed. Not one of us stopped watching the television. We checked our phones and some of us received text messages, calls, and video messages of miracles in our own families. It was after these messages when we started to disperse to get to our families. Those of us who's family members were in other cities or nations, called or video chatted with the documented miracles.

Hospitals specifically reported every person in the morgue came back to life who died within the last hour. As hospitals across the world reported their dead coming back to life, so many people began populating cemeteries to see if their loved ones came back to life. These families were disappointed. So were the families of those who passed more than an hour ago. These people did not come back to life. Just like God's servant declared. There were so many viral videos of miracles and no one watched the God's Servant Podcast Live.

The world was in awe. Hospitals and clinics were empty day one. Every illness and sickness was healed. Every disease and virus was instantly gone from the bodies of those suffering. Many people cried tears of joy, however, there were some who were angry at God. I watched a viral video and couldn't believe my eyes. This woman was blind, deaf, mute, and paralyzed. She had a plethora of things wrong with her health. I couldn't believe this woman was angry at God. "IT'S ABOUT FUCKING TIME GOD HEALED ME! I'VE BEEN LIKE THIS A LONG TIME. I GREW

UP IN THE CHURCH. I HAVE NEVER DID ANYTHING TO DESERVE THIS!..." "...Ms. Helen, I don't understand why you're not happy. You should be celebrating right now..." Ashley added tenderly. Ashley has been Ms. Helen's caretaker for many years. Ashley did her hair and rubbed her arms daily so she would know she's loved. Ashley couldn't talk to Ms. Helen and Ms. Helen couldn't tell Ashley anything over the years. Ashley loved her very much and kept Ms. Helen in her prayers for the last ten years. My heart was crushed when I heard, "Ms. Helen, God has given you a miracle and you're angry! You should be overjoyed right now. You should be thankful. You don't have a grateful heart and this hurts me..." Ashley walked away quickly as she began crying. The person recording the video asked Ms. Helen, "Do you feel like you deserve this healing miracle?" "YES YOU MOTHERFUCKER YES! I WAS GOOD TO EVERYONE BEFORE THIS HAPPENED TO ME! I WENT TO CHURCH FAITHFULLY AND SERVED IN

MY CHURCH! DAMN RIGHT I DESERVE THIS!" Ms. Helen shouted. The video recorder, "So now what will you do with your life? Will you go back to your church? What now? Where do you go from here?" Ms. Helen took time to think about their questions. She responded, "I honestly don't know. I just found out I've been like this ten years. I don't even know what's going on in the country, or the world for that matter. I need to think about it." Video ended. I called the hospital and asked to speak to Ashley. I explained everything I knew about the miracles and she suggested, "Come to my apartment. I'm letting Ms. Helen stay with me. Maybe she will listen to you. Give me your number..... Got it! I'll text you my address right now." My heart went out to Ms. Helen and I wanted her to know her previous condition was coming back in 40 days. I only hoped she would listen to me. We decided I would meet them at her apartment at 7pm.

Meanwhile, the world seemed as if it was turned upside down. There was mostly joy and happiness expressed by those healed of sickness and disease. It was only the first day and I believed the world would believe God did this amazing thing. Everyone in church most certainly praised God and declared the 1000 year reign of Christ has began on earth. I was clueless to whatever this meant. On the contrary, there were many new age teachers who claimed, "Humanity! We have ascended into our divine. We are now eternal beings." There were so many of these people saying this and it appeared most people were paying attention. These videos were gaining a lot of views. More views than the church videos. I watched many of these videos until it was time to meet Ashley and Ms. Helen.

I was so happy to meet someone who received a miracle. We had some small talk. Ms. Helen seemed much happier now. I was glad to see her lovely smile. Ashley was a Christian and gave God praise for healing Ms. Helen. This is when I shared my information. I asked Ashley if I could use her smart tv and mirrored my phone. I played the replay video of God's servant. Ms. Helen believed although her heart ached. The thought of being back in the same condition made her new found happiness dim. Ashley suggested, "Ms. Helen. At least you know God healed you and you have 40 days to enjoy your life. At least we know this will end, but you can make a lifetime of great memories in these 40 days. Let's do everything you ever desired, but most of all, do not be angry at God. At least you have 40 days. It could have been no days at all. I mean, look at you! You look amazing! No muscle atrophy at all." I intervened, "Ms. Helen, I desire to see you have 40 days of fun. Make your list and let's make plans immediately. No matter what it is, write it down and let's see if we can make it happen. Ok?" "Ok! Thank you Mike." Ms. Helen's response triggered Ashley to get pen and paper for her client. I'll never forget the radiance which shined on Ms. Helen as she made her list "Fun List."

Ashley turned on the news at my request. "... we just can't believe it. For those just turning in, the stock market ended the day down eight thousand with reports of all hospitals in our nation being empty. How did this happen? Pharmaceutical companies lost 800 billion today as people across the nation cancelled all prescription medications. Hospitals also lost 750 million dollars as scheduled procedures for tomorrow and beyond were also cancelled. Insurance companies started out with gains and held steady knowing there will be no payouts with so many cancelled procedures..." After hearing this information, Mike shared, "Omg! It's happening already! What God's servant said would happen is already taking place. Can I turn the channel?" Ashley allowed Mike control over the remote. He flipped until he briefly saw the The Weather Channel. As he paused for a moment, he flipped passed it, but heard, "...There's lots of rain in deserts all over the world..." "Wait? What was that?" Mike uttered feeling surprised as he flipped back to The Weather Channel. "... Let's look at this world map. Here's how it looked yesterday and here's how it is now. Now let's take a look at just a few hours ago. Look at this at 11am eastern standard time, there were no clouds over any deserts worldwide. Just 2 two hours later, precisely at 1pm eastern standard time, watch the world map over each desert. Clouds began forming over every desert at the same time. What are the odds of this? I know we've been watching and hearing miracles all day it seems worldwide, but this is also a miracle. These clouds are not moving. There is no reason or logic to why these clouds are just standing over the deserts. Over the last several hours, 6 inches of rain in every desert at the same time. That's a lot of rain! The Atacama desert in South America receives less than 0.1 cm of rain per year. The Sahara Desert gets 3 to 4 inches of rain a year. Death Valley 2 to 3 inches. Something unusual is taking place across the globe in the deserts. Other deserts are approaching its annual rainfall totals. The Kalahari Desert receives 5 to 10 inches of rain annually and the Goba Desert receives 8 inches of rain annually..." Mike believed this information was spectacular. He logged into the no named preachers podcast. He was still live. [GOD'S SERVANT] LIVE 1 watching

[0 COMMENTS]

He had no comments and once again, I was the only one watching him. He was on his face again sobbing. I logged off and focused back to the tv, "... amazing right? Now look at this. The temperature at the polar caps is dropping rapidly. Since 1pm est, the temperature has dropped 27 degrees. Let's look at it in real time. When the temperature began dipping, cloud cover also started. Look at how thick these clouds are in both hemispheres. They look identical. They appear to be moving in sync. How is this possible? I tell you, this August 2nd will go down in history and in the record books. We will know by this time tomorrow the total rainfall numbers in the deserts and if the polar caps break records as well. Back to you in the studio..."

I muted the television and focused my attention to Ashley and Ms. Helen. I decided to record the two of them. Those wonderful smiles and delightful laughs had to be captured. I had an idea, but I didn't want to interrupt this moment. Maybe Ms. Helen could learn braille. She was paralyzed from the waist down, this way she could read books and maybe write in braille. Not being able to hear, speak, see, and walk is depressing to imagine. Maybe this could help, but I didn't want to anger her. Maybe I'll bring it up later. "... Mike, ... Mike, MIKE!" Ashley repeated because he appeared to be in a focused dazed. "Huh? What?..." Mike snapped out of it. Ms. Helen and Ashley laughed as Mike's attention transitioned to their laughter. He smiled as Ms. Helen began to say, "Ashley and I were working on my list when she suggested I learn braille. I agreed immediately. What do you think Mike?" "OMG!!! I WAS THINKING THE SAME THING WHEN YOU BROKE MY THOUGHT!!! YES!!!" I was overjoyed knowing although she would be returning to her previous physical state, but at least she will have something she didn't have before to make her situation better. [GOD'S SERVANT] LIVE 0 watching

[0 COMMENTS]

"... God you really did what you said to me. I'm so sorry I doubted you." He rose off the floor and sat on his sofa looking well-pleased. "Honestly, I feel like Noah, but worse. At least Noah had an audience listening to him. No one is listening to me. I am experiencing the miraculous and know it's God at work, but the world is not giving glory to God. I took a break earlier, but you wouldn't know this, well, no one knew this. I watched a viral video of people saying, 'Humans have entered into their divine. We have become gods.' Did you see the video? If not, the link is provided below. It was unbelievable the things I heard. Please know and understand God said no one will die across the world for 40 days and 40 nights. On day 41 at noon central standard time, death will be restored into earth. God has released wholeness over the earth. Every living thing, and every ecosystem which was sick and diseased, are being healed. God is healing the land, the weather, crops, and water. Mind-boggling things will take place. You will see. Even though no one is watching me live, August 2, the day this is being recorded, will still be available for replays. This is my evidence; well, the Lord's evidence He did do this thing even if we as His creation never recognizes Him for it. However, let it be noted, this September 11th will be remembered for more than just the attack on the United States. At noon central standard time, every person who was healed, will once again be sick with which ever sickness or disease they previously possessed. I know there is one person who comes to my live. I pray you share this live with your followers. Please share. Be my Aaron. Look up Aaron and Moses if you don't understand what I'm saying to you. This will be my last live broadcast until September 10th. Those of you who are healed, enjoy your lives to the fullest and please give God the glory. Take care everyone. Jesus is Lord. God bless you."

[GOD'S SERVANT] was Live

[0 COMMENTS]

A month has passed and so much has happened in the world. We just returned from our our latest trip. We have been to Italy, France, London, and Singapore. We did "3 day weekends" in each. Tuesdays and Wednesdays were braille instruction days which Ms. Helen picked up on very quickly. We tried every restaurant Ms. Helen desired. Mr. Webb gave me time off from my job. As a matter of fact, Mr. Webb gave our entire company time off so we could all enjoy our family members who were now healed of cancer, alzheimer's, and other diseases. My family understood my quest with Ms. Helen. We were on the go so much with Ms. Helen, I didn't see if God's servant went live. I went to his social media page and to my surprise, he hasn't been live for 4 weeks. I watched the replay while Ms. Helen and Ashley took a nap.

[GOD'S SERVANT] was Live

[0 COMMENTS]

When I heard him give me a message, my eyebrows raised. I didn't know the bible at all. I looked up Aaron on the internet. I've heard of

Moses, but not Aaron. After acquiring information, I understood what God's servant desired me to do. Aaron spoke for Moses. He wanted me to speak on his behalf by sharing his broadcast to my following and instruct them to share it to their following. He had zero views until I watched it. I shared his live and added instructions.

My Mike Is On⊘   shared a video

[GOD'S SERVANT] was Live

"This is very serious. Watch and share. Also, see previous video. Get the word out!"

    Afterwards, I watched the news, something I didn't do for the last several weeks. I was so busy enjoying the memories we were making with Ms. Helen to be concerned with anything else. I funded everything without thought knowing this money went to a great cause. I turned up the volume and walked closer to the screen because I couldn't believe my eyes. "... Wowwwww! Are you seeing this David?" News Reporter Joanne asked news anchor David live on the scene in the downtown business district. David answered, "Yes! We are witnessing this with you live in the studio! We can't believe it either. Joanne, can show us another angle?" The camera man moved quickly to position the view to a new angle. "Ok. Here's a different view. This has been going on live for about 20 minutes now and the line looks like a theme park waiting crowd. For those just tuning in, ...wait a second, see for yourself..." The camera zoomed to the top of the iconic building which was the feature of our dazling cities skyline. There were two white guys standing on the edge looking down momentarily and high-fiving each other repeatedly as the crowd behind them cheered them on before saying, "5...4...3...2...1... JUMP!!!!!" They jumped up together falling 1300 feet to the street. As if they were superheros, they both stood up without injury high-fiving and chest bumping. Joanne and her camera man ran over to them. "Guys!!! Guys!!! Can you please talk to me?" Sure one said as the other nodded in agreement. "Why are you jumping off buildings?" She asked seriously yet in wonder they actually did it. "First of all, Joanne, I'm a fan. My name is Cal-El. I'm superman..." The guy with him interrupted, "... No you're not, I'm Cal-El." They both started arguing on live television. Joanne intervened, "Guys please stop, stop, guys..." They both settled down. "Please answer this one question: why did you jump off a skyscraper?" They both responded almost simultaneously, **"BECAUSE WE ARE ETERNAL BEINGS! WE CAN'T DIE!!!"** They cheered as they walked away from Joanne as 4 more individuals hit the street rising with no injuries. This time it was 4 black guys. Then 7 women of different races. I watched this in disbelief knowing on September 11th was approaching. I flipped to the other news channels. People were shooting themselves with guns, people tried to stab themselves, and some drank poison. No one died. I never dreamed these things could take place. I kept watching different news sources which shared similar situations. People were claiming to be God. All over the world various races of people were claiming they were divine. Very few people outside of Christians gave God the glory due unto His name. As I watched the news, Ashley touched my shoulder breaking my focus. I muted the television. "Mike, what were you watching?" I informed Ashley. Ms. Helen joined us 10 minutes later. We shared the information. We were all dumbfounded. I unmuted the television to hear, "Hospitals and clinics throughout the world are on the verge of closing. Everyone is losing money. All medical stocks have dropped 98% in the last month. Mike knowing what was going to happen next, stepped outside to call his stockbroker and bought shares in the thousands in multiple medical companies. Even though he spent thousands on Ashley and Ms. Helen, Mike still had just under a million dollars in his savings. He didn't inform them or anyone else of this. Now he had just over two hundred thousand left in his savings. His stockbroker tried to stop him, but Mike already knew the outcome and purchased freely.

As Mike returned to Ashley and Ms. Helen, he suddenly had a thought to turn to The Weather Channel. Ms. Helen and Ashley were talking about our next trip to South Africa. "... I'm beyond happy to be live on the scene here in what used to be the Sahara Desert. Where did all of the vegetation come from? There are full beautiful lakes. Oh wow! A fish just jumped out of the water. How did fish get here? There are biologist out here, but they declined talking to us. They didn't want to be disturbed. As you can see, they have their own camera crew..." I muted the television to ponder for a moment. Every desert of the world is no longer a desert. Is this God too? Could a desert be a sickness with the earth?

I turned the channel to watch other news sources. I unmuted the tv, "Insurance companies are contemplating filing bankruptcy as millions of people cancel their health and life insurance policies. On the contrary, they are actually saving millions of dollars with hospitals being empty. Insurance stocks are down, but not by much." Channel flipped, "...The polar caps have frozen over adding, rather, replacing ice that melted. Let's look at these satelite pictures in July. Now let's look at this pic taken today. This is a lot of ice! If this continues, in the next 7 days, all of the ice will be replaced with new ice restoring the polar caps. What is taking place in the earth?..." Channel flipped, "... police are saying crime has changed over the last month. Since people are not dying, no one has been giving up their possessions. Armed robberies are useless now. In addition, police arrests are down too for the same reason. Weapons have become useless since people can't be hurt anymore." Television off.

Ms. Helen sits near me smiling. "Mike, I just want to thank you for everything. You've been so kind and I appreciate all you've done for me, and Ashley. During my nap, I had a dream and this dream touched my heart. In my dream, I saw myself laying in the hospital. I still had my hearing although it was very bad. Ashley asked me to make my requests known unto God in prayer. She informed me God hears my heart although I couldn't speak. I completely forgot this prayer. I actually prayed, 'Lord, please heal me and allow me to enjoy my life. I've been good to people and I would like to make a few good memories before I die. In Jesus name I pray. Amen.' My prayer has been answered. I never had children and once I was hospitalized, well, the few family members I had passed while I was sick. No one could inform me because I couldn't hear and couldn't read braille. I'm so grateful to Ashley rubbing my arm and hair sometimes. Although I know I'm returning to my condition, I'm very happy to have experienced these trips and meals you've provided. I pray God blesses you Mike for your generosity." She tapped my knee smiling before rising up to prepare for our dinner date at a local 5 star restaurant. I brought my attire with me and I changed along with them. We shared a very fun elegant evening together.

After dropping them off, I headed to my apartment. I called my family and shared our experience with Ms. Helen. My family and I had some good laughs during our conversation. It was good to see my family spending time together although I wasn't present. I'm very pleased they all agreed I should help Ms. Helen. This just makes me love them more.

After arriving in my apartment, I decided to check my social media. I couldn't believe I only had 5 views and no shares. I logged out. I took a hot shower and prepared for bed. I admit, I now believed in God. Everything God's servant said would happen is happening. Most of the world do not credit God with the miracle of no deaths and healings across the globe. They believe we've ascended and are now gods. Every type of religion was giving credit to their god(s), but the large majority of the world believed these new age teachings, believing humanity were now eternal beings. They believed this proved we didn't need salvation through Jesus Christ. Some even declared this proved the bible isn't real. What was the answer for entire ecosystems being restored along with the ice caps? I turned my television on to The Weather Channel and lowered the volume. Commercials were playing and I stretched out waiting for their regular programing. I fell asleep before the ads ended.

"... ocean levels continue to drop as the polar caps refreeze. You don't notice it unless you live in certain areas in the world which display a clear difference. However, this is not the case in every area. We simply cannot explain why a few areas are obviously lower than before, but in my opinion, the Mediterranean Sea lowering only on the side of Egypt is very unusual. This is live footage. Look at this. How is this possible? This is Alexandria. The depth is nothing like other areas of the sea, but you can walk on dry ground. The people you see down there are Egyptologists. They have been excavating Egyptian artifacts for years prior to this day, but now, they have no water or weather to hinder them. The ground being completely dry is what surprises me. The weather isn't very hot. It's comfortable. None of this makes sense to me. What is it this generation says, 'Make it make sense.' Please make it make sense. They have been bringing out artifacts all night and day. They are afraid the water will

return so they have 24 hour shifts with continuous efforts. I interviewed one of the Egyptologists, and they shared, 'We are absolutely speechless by this event. We are discovering too many artifacts to count. The numbers keep changing every hour..."
I woke up watching The Weather Channel. I sat there watching and taking mental notes. I was about to turn the channel when... "Wait a minute? We have a breaking news story coming in now! Excuse us as we go to our affiliate network in South America. "We are live here in the Amazon Rainforest and we are mesmerized by what we our seeing. Trees have fully grown overnight. Areas which we cleared of trees now have full grown trees. No new growth. Deforestation stopped when everyone was healed worldwide. These workers have returned to full forests. All of the work they accomplished is gone. It looks as if they were never here. But that's not the crazy part. Watch this video. As you can see they are using equipment to push this tree over, and the tree is not budging. Look at this! Wow! Nothing they do is working.

When I say I have no words, I have no words. We will have more for you later. Back to the studio..."

I couldn't believe my eyes, or ears for that matter. The whole planet has been healed by God and no one is giving God the credit. Too many unexplained events have taken place. As I pondered on the information I just witnessed, my mobile phone rang. "Hello Mr. Webb. How are you?" "... Mike, did you see the text message I sent you?" "No sir, what's going on?" I replied. "Turn to channel 170 now!" I turned my television to watch breaking news. There was a serious accident taking place. A cruise ship had an explosion and rapidly sunk. No one acquired life vests because they believed they would not die. Currently there were no bodies found. The Coast Guard has sent unmanned subs searching for the wreckeage. "Mr. Webb, how long has this been happening?" "I'm not sure Mike. Do you think these people are dead?" "Honestly, I don't know. Not dying was supposed to last until September 11th. Maybe something has changed?" We began watching together in silence. Maybe the miracle ended. If it did end early, why? I got off the phone with Mr. Webb and logged into God's Servant Podcast. He wasn't live. As I scrolled in my phone, "... Look at this? Omg, do you see this? Our first sub has found the wreckage and I'm not trying to be funny, but everyone looks like Aquaman and mermaids. (Laughing) Are these the Atlantians? (More laughter) Everyone is alive! The pressure of the ocean has not effected them. Wait! I'm just realizing this: THEY HAVE NO OXYGEN!!! This is quite remarkable I must say. These people are smiling and laughing as they slowly make their way back up to the surface. If it wasn't for the subs light, we wouldn't even see them. Maybe we really are eternal beings after seeing this..." Once again, I'm amazed. Only God could do this, but no one gave Him credit. This situation encouraged more people to do more impossible things. Now people wanted to race to the bottom of the ocean. Along with people jumping off cliffs and mountain tops, now we have another foolish event added. I received a text from Ashley saying, "Start packing Mike. We have to be at the airport in 4 hours." I'm glad I asked her to remind me. There were many distractions on the news and abroad. I silenced my phone and turned my tv off. I started packing in peace and couldn't wait to see South Africa.

Ms. Helen loved everything we did on our trip. She was too thrilled. We took many pictures together and shared plenty of laughs. I hated when we had to leave. Now that we have returned, the reality is really hitting home. With only a few days remaining before everything returns, our smiles dimmed a bit. Instead of excitement while learning braille, we could specifically see a shift taking place. However, Ms. Helen took a small break and went for a walk alone. When she came back, she sat us both down. "Ashley and Mike. You've made this month very memorable for me. I couldn't have imagined anything greater than what's you've given me. I'll always treasure these memories. I took a walk because I wanted to talk to God. I apologized to Him for cursing and blaming Him for my situation. He didn't have to give me this month, but He did. I cried tears of gratefulness and after shedding those tears, I soon realized, heaven is better than this." Water began welling in her eyes. She looked far from sad. There was no sorrow. Only appreciation. The same warmth I remembered from God's Servant Podcast returned. Peace and a great feeling of being loved was present among the three of us. Ashley smiled as she declared, "The presence of God is here with us now." I thought..., well, I didn't know what to think. Ashley grabbed me by my hand, "Mike, God sent you to us. We couldn't have accomplished any of these things without you. God has a plan for your life Mike. He's going to show you. Ms. Helen, God is pleased with the change in your heart. What a powerful thing to say, 'heaven is better than this.' God reminded you of your reward Ms. Helen. I love God..." As Ashley talked tears fell from my eyes. I couldn't believe I was crying. I can't explain it, but I felt I was loved and I knew I wasn't perfect either. I was loved by God. I am loved by God. Do you fell a gentle warmth? "Ms. Helen responded with a confident, "Yes." I got down on my knees for the first time ever in my life and I cried an ocean thanking God for loving me. "That's it Mike, worship the Lord." Ashley expressed with both of her hands high in the air. We stayed in this place for more than an hour. I didn't know anything, but Ashley understood and expounded on everything which took place with us when it was over.

I logged into my social media account. I went live. This time my followers jumped on.

My Mike Is On ⊘ is LIVE 1,422 watching

"Greetings everyone, My Mike Is On (finger tap tap on his microphone) As you know the world has experienced unprecedented miracles. However, it's going to end on September 11th at noon central standard time. This incredible experience was executed by God. The God of the bible. Please look at my previous video and follow the instructions I gave with it.

My Mike Is On ⊘ is LIVE 8,297 watching

[188 COMMENTS]

[475 SHARE(S)]

Please take heed and warn everyone. Get the word out. Even if you don't believe me, tell them anyway. Share it anyway. That's all I had to say. Take care. My Mike Is Off."

My Mike Is On◉ was Live.

This time I had my usual crowd and usual numbers. I kept monitoring my video stats throughout the day and my numbers were consistently increasing. I was happy to know this, but will people believe?

Well, today is September 11th. Ms. Helen, Ashley, and myself went out to eat breakfast. Ashley slipped Ms. Helen a small pamphlet. It was about 10 pages. We were quiet this morning. Ms. Helen read her pamphlet and thanked Ashley. Over these last few days, we all purposely stayed away from the news and other information stations. We desired to be completely present with Ms. Helen. We didn't desire to discuss anything outside of our trio. After our early breakfast, we went to the museum to spend a few hours before I drove them back to the hospital. The museum was full of smiling faces and pleasant looking people. Although I tried to keep my mind present, my focus strayed to the agony which was coming. Our former reality was returning. Crime, sickness, and every other despressing thing that can cause smiles to deminish. Ms. Helen wrapped her arm in mine which brought me back. Each exhibit caused Ms. Helen to beam with joy. Although she knew what was coming for her, she was entirely confident heaven was better.

As we listened to the information at an Egyptian Exhibit, a staff member ran over to us purely thrilled to inform, "Omg!!! We have a breaking discovery right now in Egypt! New historic hieroglphics have been unearthed. I can't wait for us to learn more about Egypt." They left as swiftly as they arrived. Everyone smiled or demonstrated excitement except me as my eyes observed the time on my watch. Ms. Helen lifted my head saying, "Mike, it's ok. Really, it's ok. I want you to have joy because of the happiness you brought me. You didn't have to come to the hospital that day, but you did. Because of your caring heart, you did. Thank you. Please don't feel bad for me and don't you go blaming God like I did, ok?" As she laughed with the sun shining on her face from the nearby exit doors we were approaching.

We departed the museum with 45 minutes remaining before noon central standard time. We only needed 10 minutes. Nonetheless, Ms. Helen desired enough time to meet those who would be caring for her. Moreover, she joked, "I want first dibs on a private room." We all exploded into a deep laugh which I knew I needed. Ms. Helen was in good spirits. It was calming to see her with this present attitude; unlike before.

When we arrived at the hospital, we explained our situation and they looked at us as if we were crazy. These were nurses Ashley didn't know. Ashley grabbed a phone and made a call. Several nurses came out of nowhere and excorted us without question leaving those other nurses confused. We took the elevator to the 12th floor and

Ms. Helen picked out her own private room. This room had wonderful views of the sun rising. Ms. Helen chose this room because she wanted to feel the sun on her face in the mornings. This was so she would know it was a new day.

I had her suitcase full of new clothing she desired from every trip and some local stores. Ashley was talking with her employees. I couldn't hear them, but I could tell by their body language, they were skeptical to whatever it was Ashley was relaying. When Ashley returned to us, she expressed, "As I talked to my team members, it dawned on me this hospital is going to be full within hours. I told them to get their game faces on because it's going to be a long day." I honestly didn't desire to experience the chaos, but I didn't want to leave Ms. Helen who was going over her braille. In addition, she had a list Ashley and her created with things she wanted while, well, you know. They created hand signals and the list will be on the wall so all staff would be aware.

Ashley decided to lead us in prayer after we

made sure Ms. Helen was comfortable in her bed. She wasn't officially admitted, but we knew she would be. Ashley prayed and the loving warmth surrounded us. Ms. Helen thanked God for Mike, Ashley, and an outstanding month of dreams being fulfilled. "I love you Lord and thank you again. I love you Mike. I love you Ashley. God, bless them for me. In Jesus name. Amen." Noon arrived 2 second later. I could see Ms. Helen's eyes lose focus as her body slowly changed before our eyes. She was now physically smaller and I could tell she didn't control her legs any more. She was already laying in her bed with the back raised up at thirty degrees. Ashley immediately began rubbing her arm and I rubbed the other arm. Tears fell down Ms. Helen's face as her former reality reestablished itself. However, this situation was better than before. I sat in a seat next to her bed rubbing her arm. Ms. Helen tried to wrap her arm around mine. I aided her. I laid next to her. Our arms were now wrapped and she laid her head on my shoulder. Ashley ran out as calls to the nursing station sounded. I knew what was happening. Screech!!! I heard an accident. Then another, and another, and another. I started hearing sounds which weren't activated over the last 40 days. I could hear screams of fear and terror at street level. The familiar sound of sirens resonated through the skyline as they drew closer. The television had breaking news on it. I didn't bother turning up the volume. My mobile phone vibrated. I looked and answered with my right hand while my left arm was still wrapped with Ms. Helen's arm, "Mike, thank you for warning us to return. Your grandparents are doing well. It's not as bad as it was before because they ate better and exercised over the last month. We will keep you informed. Are you ok?" My brother Tom asked after he updated me on our family. "I'm ok. I'm with Ms. Helen right now. We had her here early..." I decided to video chat with him and we had a long talk as we filled in the blanks.

Death returned. People who were risen from the dead died while they were driving and they hit other people who were also resurrected. People who didn't listen to the podcast, and people who never knew what happened, died doing their crazy stunts. Those who were racing to the bottom of the ocean bodies imploded under the pressure. These things were capture on video or happened while being live on social media. The deserts stopped receiving rain. Weather patterns shifted back to normal. The polar caps melted extremely fast within hours and those areas were back under water before nightfall. In all this, the world didn't acknowledge God.

Ms. Helen was now asleep. I received another call. I nodded, turned the channel, and turned up the volume. I listened attentively. I was now a billionaire. As a matter of fact, I became the third wealthiest person in the United States. I didn't inform anyone and I thought it was best to leave it this way. I turned the volume back down. I didn't celebrate. Heck, I didn't even smirk. I started crying. All I wanted was Ms. Helen to be healed again. Ashley dropped in briefly making sure I was ok. I assured her I was fine although the tears were very visible. She had to work mandatory overtime with the hospital filling up at a rapid pace. We knew it was coming though. All of a sudden, I grabbed my phone to log into God's Servant Podcast.

[GOD'S SERVANT] was Live.

[COMMENTS]

[0 SHARE(S)]

"Hello. God bless you. Welcome in or maybe not. (He started laughing.) This is my first live broadcast since God healed the world and if you viewed my previous broadcasts, you see God speaking to me and I proclaimed what God said He would do, and He did it. Just like He declared, the world didn't believe. Where I am now..., is in a place of faith. It's ok if no one watches me. It's ok if no one every knows my name. As long as I know God is real through Jesus Christ, I'm good. I'm well and everything will be just fine in the end. I'm now at peace seeing how powerful God is, and seeing the wonderful things He can do. Most of all, I understand life is very hard no matter who you are in humanity, but I thoroughly know that heaven is better than this..." There are those words again, "heaven is better than this." "...I'm at peace now. I'm content with life and everything now..." I paused it. Hearing his words caused me to have a thought. "What if..."

(To Be Continued In Volume 2)

- DEPRIVATION -

STORY THREE

* * *

"EVERYONE!!!, HOW DID YOU LIKE YOUR TOUR?!!!" The tour guide Jeff shouted in the microphone as they prepared to exit their unique designed tour guide air vehicle. It looked like a combination of helicopter and airplane. It was specifically designed so individuals could see clearly from underneath to take pictures and video. This vehicle was very quick and could manuver in various ways instantly, including evasive maneuvers and countermeasures. It seated 20 people comfortably.

The 20 people who took the tour began to cheer and clap their hands. Jeff asked, "Does anyone have any questions? Several hands were raised and Jeff pointed to a woman. She asked, "I loved the L.A. Tour today, I was wondering when is the next New York City Tour?" Jeff answered, "The next

New York City Tour is a week from now and it's full... She interrupted Jeff, "...If anyone cancels please let me know. I'll leave my information with you." Jeff pointed to a man, "L.A. was crazy! But, I loved it. I still can't believe my eyes. It's so shocking to see, but worth every penny..." "Jeff asked, "...Do you have a question sir?" "Oh, ah, no not really." The man replied looking a bit embarrassed for some reason. Jeff looked at an older gentleman and nodded. The older gentleman detailed, "I used to live in L.A. It was such an amazing place at one time. I was a young man in those days. My question Jeff is this, 'If someone gets sick on the tour vehicle, how long until medical assistance arrives?'" "Well sir, umm, well, there is no medical response team. No one is coming for us. It's just too dangerous and risky. We will have to return. Meanwhile, we do have medical supplies onboard. I'm licensed, as well as others, who work here to provide some basic medical help. This is why you have to take a physical prior to our tour. We do turn people down based on their health." The older gentleman adds, "So is it safe to say, we are on our own if anything happens including malfunctions?" Jeff's facial expression was one to remember just before he uttered, "Our tours are looked down upon and if something happens, no one is coming. This is why you guys have so much paperwork to fill out. You do read your paperwork? I hope you understand the risks prior to our tour. New York is the most dangerous tour of all. I do not fly that route. There are too many unknowns, but Chad loves going to New York. He doesn't even use the drones to go ahead to make sure everything is safe. You saw me use our drones on our tour. He's better than me. Are there anymore questions? No..., ok. Everyone, thank you for choosing Memory Lane Tours. See you next time."

Uncle Sam is dead. Capitalism rest in peace. The day the USA ended was a 9/11 type of day. Those who saw it coming left the United States before it collapsed. The richest people moved out of the United States as taxes were increased on them at shocking rates. Not only did they move, but they gave up their citizenship and took their businesses, technology, and resources with them. As the top five percent of the United States became citizens of other nations, taxes on the middle class skyrocketed. The middle class couldn't afford to live basic lives. Small businesses suffered as taxes were causing them to go in the red. The businesses who could leave the United States pulled out just before all the major cities burned. Some didn't have the chance to have a going out of business sale. They closed their doors because of crime. Crime was so bad the employees quit while the criminals robbed their stores. Illegal immigrants left the United States as every priviledge was taken away from them. Every state and city government program ended. No more section 8. No more food stamps, link, or ebt. The people suffered without aid. Things went back to how the world was before The Great Depression. There was no government assistance of any kind for anyone. Nothing for women, children, or the homeless. Single mothers couldn't feed their children. There was nothing freely given any longer; even federal grants stopped altogether.

Democratic states collapsed first. As people moved out of Democratic states to Republican states, crime increased in Republican states. The wealthy residents of Republican states also relocated to other nations. Middle class families gathered their belongings and moved out of the country as well. Things were unbelievably out of control. The poorest of people had it the worst. They didn't have the resources to leave. Many Americans crossed the border into Mexico illegally. Those who were caught were put in prison, but they didn't care. It was better than being in the United States. The prison system in the United States became a cemetery. Prison guards and prison staff stopped going to work to protect their families during the chaos. This also happened with law enforcement across the nation. Fire departments, hospitals, and all social services had staff quit altogether to protect their families. No one gave two week notices. Airports were overrun with people booking one way tickets to other nations. The final blow to the United States was when airports didn't have anymore airplanes. Pilots refused to fly back to the United States. As more pilots took this stance, there were only domestic flights and pilots were practically nonexistant. Some of the few pilots who were scheduled for domestic flights, changed their flight plans to other nations. News reporters were being attacked and some were murdered live on the air. As a result, news channels didn't have anymore live broadcasts on the scene of any incident.

Many companys suddenly closed without notice and left thousands without jobs. There was no last paychecks or unemployment benefits. People became desperate and stole food from grocery stores. Once the grocery stores were empty, this is when things became chaotic. Home invasions were everyday as people searched for food. Murders became routine for most Americans. The terrible icing on the cake was when calling 911 no one answered. Every part of the United States was lawless. Even when the President of the United States tried to use the military to bring peace and safety back to the country, it was already too late. More than half of the military went awol to check on their parents, spouses, and children. Those who found their families brought them back to military bases. No charges were brought to these soldiers because the United States needed them. The military superiors understood and actually sent those same soldiers on missions to retrieve their own families. These soldiers were given orders to protect their families at all costs. They were given all of the resources they needed. Other nations thought to invade the United States, but the president said, "Any nation who attacks or invades us while we are dealing with our situation, we will nuke your nation. We are willing to destroy the entire planet being that we have nothing to lose currently." The United States nuclear subs were positioned strategically against most nations. The missiles could reach any target in 5 minutes or less. One nation showed aggresion to the United States.

They sent their naval fleets, but before they could get anywhere close to the United States, a tactical nuke was sent against this nation. It's target was where their political leaders met which was empty. The nuke was small enough to only destroy this target without destroying the entire nation. This nation learned a valuable lesson. Their fleet returned and no one else showed aggression. Honestly, they didn't need to show any. The United States imploded and destroyed itself.

All that's left of the United States are a few U.S. Embassy locations in a few countries. These lasted many years until there wasn't a reason to keep them anymore. There was no money. As resources depleted, these closed permanently without notification. This was very embarrasing for all proud U.S. citizens, who were also hunted and killed in some countries where the U.S. was hated. No nations came to assist the United States. This was very painful to witness. The U.S. helped many nations that turned their backs on us when we needed them the most. No aid or resources were ever offered by any allied nation.

The President of the United States was in hiding as most of the 50 states were filled with turmoil. When some of the 50 states disbanded from the United States, and became sovereign nations, this was when we all knew it was over. The remaining patriotic citizens of the United States knew the fight to save the country was over. They also departed the United States. Most of them left in tears knowing it was the end. The only news sources were those who went live on social media showing the disorder in every city. The mayors disappeared in cities which no longer had law enforcement or national guard. Mobs of people burned the mayors homes. Landmarks burned. Downtown buildings had multiple floors on fire. Dead bodies were not recovered by anyone. Men, women, and children were victims of horrible crimes. One entire family, (husband, wife, two daughters, and a son) were all abused together live on social media. There was a crowd of heavily armed individuals waiting their turn to abuse each member of this family. Anyone trying to help them was shot dead instantly, but some were forcefully restrained and became abuse victims with the family. This disgusting live video from New York City was the last live broadcast. We didn't know if the cell towers went down, or if the power went out. As other cities had live videos displaying criminals in the act, they too went dark like New York until there were no more news, live videos, or communication coming from the United States.

Once America was entirely dark, other nations advanced to invade the U.S.. The President, of what was left of the United States, addressed the world when the enemies of the United States approached. Once again, these nations militaries returned because of the threat with nuclear weapons. Even though the nation was destroyed from within, the President still protected the land.

The United States citizens who lived off of the grid were unaware the country collapsed. People who escaped the cities occupied areas with crops, or stayed in forests within their states. As more and more people did this, the criminals also followed once there was nothing or no one in the big cities. Some African Americans were found lynched. Men, women, and children were found dead naked. Some parents hid their children. Unfortunately, these children witnessed the abuse their parents endured together. Many children watched their single mother be abused as they hid in the distance. With no food and no skills to hunt or survive, asking anyone for help was a risk. Some people had to trade their bodies for food for their children. Desperation changed the characters of decent people. Some were changed for the good of others. With no law enforcement anywhere to be found, a few heros arose who lived off the grid. They saved many families and killed criminals in the families defense. Once they knew the United States no longer existed, they informed others who lived off the grid and together formulated plans to leave the former U.S.. These strategically armed heros had radios to inform Canada, or Mexico, who they were, and what they were doing.

Fortunately, most of these people still possessed their identification and passports. The federal government shared all United States cititizens data with Mexico and Canada to identify the good citizens from the criminals. When the smoke cleared, there was nothing left of the former United States of America, but empty buildings, some landmarks, and remnants of its former greatness. One year later, Memory Lane Tours was created by a wealthy business person. This person purposely remained in the shadows to avoid anyone knowing their identity. This person possessed the resources to build the special tour vehicles and pay a hefty price for adventurous pilots who dared to fly into the former United States. Our owner never visited our office. They only contacted us via email. They always ended the email with the signature reading, "By all means, Keep Up the great work. GCD." We were located in downtown Regina Canada.

Canada built a fortified wall around its border with armed soldiers to keep the criminals from the

United States from entering. The new rule was to shoot onsight without facing consequences. In the aftermath of the United States falling apart, Canada did not want to lose one person to anyone crossing the border illegally. Every border employee was to go home to their families. There were designated places to enter Canada legally. If you tried any other way, death was your sentence. It didn't matter if you were a woman with children either. Females murdered several Canadian Border Patrol Agents acting as if they were victims of violence and rape. Young children also killed Canadian Border Patrol Agents. After sixteen deaths, Canadian lawmakers had enough. Everyone dies onsight. No exceptions! Warning signs were everywhere. Even the people who couldn't read knew the visual meaning of these signs. After Canadians, and the news world, watched the videos of women and children killing border patrol agents, everyone in Canada had enough! The wall had bright lighting so anyone could be seen up to a quarter of a mile away. All trees and bushes were destroyed so there were no hiding places. The bodies of the dead were not removed in hopes it would prevent anyone from trying to cross illegally. All boats were thoroughly searched on all waterways and oceans. Curfews were in place on all waters and soldiers patrolled with special gun boats. Anyone with illegal United States citizens were shot on sight. No questions. No arrests. As sad as it was on both sides, this was the world we now lived in. Trust no one from the former United States. The law was almost reversed, but a woman who looked like she was fleeing from a group of men, ran toward the border illegally with two young children. The Border Patrol Agent was working alone that night and didn't shoot anyone onsight. Amy, the Border Patrol Agent, yelled to the woman to keep running toward the wall. Amy was about to open a section of the wall when the woman, and her children, started shooting at Amy. The men chasing her also started shooting. Amy was shot nine times, but pressed a button calling for backup. A section of the wall opened and those shooting thought they were about to enter, but there were hidden machine guns which sprayed the men, the mother, and her children to death. Amy died as help arrived. After this incident, death onsight was solidified forever. Citizens of the U.S. in other nations hated this law. The fact of the matter is, U.S. citizens were victims of many things in other nations. The realization they were no longer protected by the Constitution of the United States was a strong reality check. Many didn't know the laws of other nations and were put in prison for things they could freely do in the U.S.. While in prison, the understanding that "no one is coming to help me" humbled Americans across the globe. Although Americans hated this shoot onsight law, they understood they do not have a country anymore. No one lives crossing illegally from the United States. Only the worse and most evil people remained in the ruins of the former United States.

"Hey Jeff, are you ready for the new recruit?" His coworker Tiffany asked. "What new recruit? No one told me anything about a new recruit." "She will be here today to train with you." "Not today Tiffany. I'm scheduled for training recertifications myself." Jeff explained as the new recruit Mercedes walked in. She was a former pilot in the United States Airforce who went awol. When Jeff saw her face he was in love with her cuteness. Tiffany introduced herself to Mercedes, and introduced her to Chad, Jeff, and Porsche. All of them were awol from the United States military branches who either flew airplanes, helicopers, or both. Jeff informed Mercedes, "Well, you were supposed to be with me today, but I have training recertifications. Today you will be doing flight simulations to each of the U.S. cities we tour over." "Ok." Mercedes answered ready to get started. Jeff walked her into the simulation training room and was about to explain the controls when she said, "Controls look easy enough. I see you combined helicoper and airplane panels." "Good eye. Well, let me show you how to get started. You'll learn everything in one day and you'll start in flight training tomorrow." Jeff tried everything he could not to gaze at her beauty. "Thanks." Mercedes stated out of nowhere. "Why are you thanking me?" Jeff asked curiously. She gently smiled at him, "Well, I see you find me attractive, but you're very respectful. It's nice to experience this." Jeff started turning red as he blushed at her smile. He was a handsome man with perfect teeth. The nerdy geek image he used to have was shreaded as he learned style and manly grooming tips. Jeff had the look women wanted without the games of alpha males. He was always too nice for the few women he tried to date, and he was full of morality causing him to stay away from cheap sex. He was a very good preserved man untouched by social media awareness. Jeff never went to church, but most people considered him a saint. As they went back and forth talking, their manager, Kevin, entered the simulation training room. "Jeff, I see you met Mercedes. Your recertifications training is canceled. You have the best safety record. No violations, or close calls, you're recertified Jeff as of now. Take Eagle 5, it just passed inspection and fully fueled. Show her the evasive maneuver systems and the first aid kit. Be back by lunch. I will have a meeting afterwards..." "...Wait, what meeting? I didn't see any meetings on the itinerary today." "It's a surprise meeting. I've received some news everyone needs to hear together. Be back by lunch. Oh, do not fly into the former U.S. today under no circumstances. This is what the meeting is concerning." Kevin walks away to leave the room as Jeffs adds, "Kevin? Should we have the meeting now? Everyone is here." "It can wait til after lunch. Be on time you guys." They all exited the simulation room together. Kevin went to the right while Jeff and Mercedes turned left.

As they exited their facility in downtown Regina on 13th Avenue. They headed west to the Regina International Airport where their tour vehicles were located. On tour days, they operated exactly like airlines. Mercedes asked Jeff a question breaking the silence as they passed King Street, "What's on your mind Jeff? You are definitely zoned out on something." Jeff took a moment to sort his thoughts, "Well, I'm wondering about this meeting today. We never have surprise meetings. I'm just..., I'm just a bit worried about this. I hope we are not going out of business." "I'm sure it's not that serious Jeff." Mercedes stated trying to comfort him. Jeff slowed the car down to briefly look at the water in Wascana Creek, as he turned his blinker on to make a left on Sandra Schmirler Way. He took this time to explain their companies hanger location and how airport safety worked. He turned right on Airport Road and headed to their hangar.

After the security check points, Mercedes and Jeff were cleared to depart with Eagle 5 in one hour. This gave Jeff enough time to orientate her to the craft before departure. They could lift straight up or taxi to take off, whichever was more convenient. He explained the controls which she understood quickly. The evasive maneuvers were a bit tricky, but she understood instantly. "This is absolutely incredible! The military could have used this vehicle! These maneuvers could have saved plenty of lives if this was available..." Jeff interupted Mercedes, "... Ok! Ok! I need you present now in this moment! Ok?" She calmed down realizing the trauma she experienced during the meltdown of the United States was triggered. There was a large group of armed people who were prepared to attack the U.S. military. They called themselves "SuperNova." Their vision was in their name. They desired to destroy the 50 stars and saturate the 13 stripes with the blood of Americans. No one truly knows what happened to this group. They took heavy loses once the Navy found and targeted their bases with their latest long range weapon. Prior to the Navy intervening, many soldiers were lost in the battle against them as they tried to keep the peace in major cities. This also contributed to soldiers go awol seeing such a great organized trained resistance against the government. No one knows if they still exist, and if they did exist, how are they being sustained? Mercedes knew many soldiers in the Army and the Marines who lost their lives against SuperNova. She was part of a group of soldiers who tracked and fought against SuperNova. This battle led to both sides retreating with no clear victor. Her trauma was triggered, but Jeff helped her calm and refocus.

After their taxi take off, Jeff took this time to explain everything again. When they reached their designated training area, he demonstrated evasive maneuvers in real time. She picked up on them quickly and mimicked exactly what Jeff showed her. If their craft was hit and they were going down, he gave her valuable information about the ejection seats. The ejection seats propelled the pilots from the side. If ejected upwards, the special blades would kill them instantly. Passenger ejection seats also propelled them from the side. If the vehicle was in a spin, it would be very dangerous to eject. Parachutes were intergrated into every seat and automatically activated 75 feet from their vehicle. After practicing various evasive maneuvers, they landed in their designated resting area. Here is where Jeff showed her the First Aid Kit (Fakt). There were two very big metal boxes on each side of the vehicle. Jeff said, "If we ever need anything from the first aid kit, say 'Fakt check.'" Everyone aboard will know what you're saying. "These are some very big boxes for first aid. Why are they so big?" Mercedes questioned feeling a bit uncertained of what the answer might be." "Well, if we are hurt, or injured, no one is coming to help us. We are going to need all the first aid to survive our situation. Understood?" Jeff shared as he placed his fist out. "Understood." Mercedes replied as she lifted her fist. They fist bumped as they prepared to return to their office for the meeting. Jeff took notice she didn't actually open neither first aid kit.

They walked into the conference room which was prepared for their meeting. Kevin looked uncomfortable as everyone walked in on time. Everyone was present: Chad, Porsche, Tiffany, Bruce, Chuck, Jeff, and Mercedes. Kevin had folders at each seat as he began informing his pilots, "This is the latest information on the former United States. Satellite images show a large group of people we believe are SuperNova, moving from West Virginia heading Northeast. We believe they are heading toward New York. We believe this is the entirety of what remains of their group. Looks like almost three hundred people. As you can see from these pictures, they are heavily armed. Luckily they do not have greater numbers. For now, we are going to cancel our tours to New York City." Chad was very upset at this information and declared, "Why stop going to New York City because of these fools? New York is a very big city and we can use the drones to avoid these people. If we cancel, we are losing millions of dollars." "Exactly! I couldn't have said it better." Bruce supported Chad his co-pilot to New York City (NYC). "This group of people have rocket launchers, and we cannot risk lives to make money..." Kevin expressed as his concerning words were broken by Porsche, "...Why cancel New York? We are train pilots and our evasive maneuvers are second to none! I was looking forward to piloting this tour." The NYC Tour was about to receive a second tour day Porsche was going to Pilot with Chuck who was also a new recruit just finishing his training and certifications. The next tour to NYC was scheduled to depart in three days. Kevin insisted the tour be canceled and sent out email notifications of the tour cancelation before the meeting ended, but they also had the option to change to the Chicago Tour which was scheduled in four days. As the meeting progressed, everyone notified changed to the Chicago Tour option. The tension this meeting possessed during the NYC portion subsided as they talked about other concerns. After discussing a few safety issues, the meeting was over. Kevin asked Mercedes about her training away from everyone. She was very confident about working here. Then he asked Jeff about her training in like manner. She received very good remarks from Jeff. Based on this, she was approved for next day fly over tour simulations and some safety rule exams. If she passed, she would be assigned a smaller tour to begin.

Chad and Bruce walked out while everyone still talked after the meeting. They went back and forth with each other until they agreed to change the tour from Chicago to NYC. They went immediately to the airport and carefully changed the itinerary, in a strong effort no confirmations were needed to be sent by email. Instead of Eagle 4, Eagle 12 would be their tour vehicle with more fuel capacity. Eagle 5 through 12 were the vehicles used for the NYC Tour, and other tours which went deep into the former United States. Chad and Bruce completed everything without the consent from their manager Kevin. They knew they were risking their jobs, but they didn't care. Both of them had safety violations on their records, however, it was nothing to this magnitude. They made sure not to inform the customers of the tour change. They would say it was a surprise after embarking for Chicago. Bruce specifically told Chad, "We do not need anyone emailing or calling Kevin with questions." Chad agreed. They went back to the office to find everyone still talking. There was literally nothing else to do after the meeting. Everyone was on salary. No one made any overtime. This is detailed in their individual contracts.

As everyone left work for the day, Jeff waited until everyone was separated from Mercedes and himself. "There's a nice spot called Famoso Italian Pizzeria, would you like to get something to eat?" "Jeff, are you asking me out on a date?" Mercedes questioned tilting her head to the side and looking up at him smiling. "Ah, yes, yes I am asking you out on a date." He released feeling like this went very well. "Ok, let's go." Mercedes answered. She followed him in her car. They had a wonderful evening together. Everything was perfect: the food, the drinks, and the dessert. She finally asked, "I have to bring this back up. This has been on my mind all day. Why are those first aid kits enormous?" She released a big laugh as she leaned into Jeff's chest with her beautiful straight white teeth. She continued as she positioned herself upright in her seat, "Please explain sir." Jeff's smile weakened as his face contorted to a more serious look, "Honestly, we've never used it, but I opened one just to see what was inside." Jeff became quiet. "Well Jeff, don't leave me hanging." "Well,

Mercedes, ... it's full of weapons. Military guns, grenades, C4, and much more. That's why it's so big. We are all from the military, and in the case we crashed, or had any mechanical issues, we were to fight our way out." "Are you kidding me? Does anyone else know they have weapons aboard?" "I don't think so. When I found out, I went to Kevin who told me to keep quiet about it, but there's more." "What do you mean, more?" "Within the first aid kit is an activation button to initiate onboard weapon systems. Kevin had each vehicle integrated secretly. This is one reason why he respects me so much because I took the time to check the entire tour vehicle. Wait, we have just enough time to get to the hangar if you want to see..." "...No, it can wait until tomorrow. I'm enjoying our time together. Can we just stay here, please?" She uttered with a very sweet voice as she eased her way slowly toward him. She touched his chin softly and turned it toward her face. She gave Jeff a tender kiss then pulled away from him. Jeff was very happy the woman he liked also liked him.

They had a few more drinks and continued talking about many things. Some were job related, but they shared many personal things. Things which led to them holding hands before the night ended.

The next morning, Mercedes and Jeff met at the hangar and thoroughly searched the first aid kits on each tour vehicle. They recognized many of the weapons. Jeff activated the onboard weapon systems to see what happened. Another panel opened to the left, and another to the right, which weren't there before. They both sat down in their pilot seat and looked over the weapon panels. The two seated tour vehicles had weapons operated by each pilot separately. Each had front and rear separate weapons. The left seat had leftsided weapons and the right had rightsided weapons. The single seat tour vehicles, for shorter distance tours, had a bigger panel operating all weapons in the front, the rear, and the sides. Jeff and Mercedes walked around each tour vehicle visually acknowledging each weapons location. Jeff had never seen them before. "Jeff, who created these tour vehicles?" She asked feeling as if something very suspicious was in the works. "I wish I knew. Maybe Kevin has the answers we're looking for. Let's ask him when we get to work. These vehicles were created for more than just tours. These are war machines." After their serious conversation, they headed to work in silent deep thought.

As they entered the office, they went straight to Kevin who looked as if he was in deep thought himself. Jeff and Mercedes both stood in Kevin's office in silence as they watched him, at his desk with his head down, with both hands on his head. Kevin looked up and wasn't surprised by their presence. "What's going on Kevin?" Jeff asked. Kevin didn't respond as his head went back down and he placed his hands on his head again. Jeff had never witnessed Kevin with this body language before. "Kevin, you're making me nervous. Are we going out of business?" "No it's not that! Ok!?" "Ok, ok, why are you raising your voice at me?" "At us." Mercedes said after Jeff asked his question. He didn't say anything. The voices of coworkers nearby filled his office. Kevin rose up and closed his office door. "Something very bad is about to happen." Kevin shared feeling and looking scared to talk to us. "Here's what I was told by our owner. The President of the United States is about to rebuild the former United States." Kevin slid one of his desk drawers open. He pulled out a folder, opened it, and asked them to come to his side of the desk. "Here's the latest satelite photos. This is the White House. As you can see, it's fortified with the military. Here are pics of the Navy nearby in the Atlantic Ocean. The military is going to sweep through Washington D.C. to make sure all criminal activity is nullified. Any criminal threats will be killed onsight. After they reestablish D.C., they will reestablish N.Y.C.." Jeff and Mercedes were shocked and happy at the same time. "What's very bad about this Kevin?" Mercedes asked smiling with joy the United States will be restored. "Number one, we will be out of business." "Ok, that's bad. What else?" Jeff asked. "Well, I'm glad you know about the first aid kits, because you're going to use them soon." Kevin released with a big sigh of stressful fear. "What do you mean? Why?" Kevin paused and gathered his thoughts before saying, "Our tour vehicles will be used to help clearout the remaining people in the former United States. Let's say, none of you desire to fly these vehicles, they have soldiers already trained to take your place." Kevin paused again. No one asked anymore questions. They waited for Kevin to speak. "The military will go from state to state killing every person they see. It doesn't matter who they are or where they come from. As of today, anyone in the former U.S. are considered enemies and must be eliminiated..." "... YOU MEAN EXTERMINATED!!!" Mercedes screamed. This caused several people to knock on Kevin's door asking if he was ok. Kevin opened the door saying, "He's fine." No one explained why Mercedes screamed. Everyone left his office except the original three. Jeff closed his office door again. "The United States will be rebuilt almost exactly how it was first established. Little by little, the military will move through each state until all fifty states are restored. Except Hawaii. It's the only state that remained lawful. They purposely went dark to protect themselves. The U.S. military with the President have Hawaii safeguarded.

There is going to be televised speeches for Americans to come back home after each state they lived in is rebuilt." Kevin went silent again as he dropped his head momentarily and looked up at them nervously. Jeff and Mercedes didn't bother asking Kevin another question. They both knew he was going to inform them of everything at this point. "I do not want to say this to you." Kevin paused for a minute trying to gather his words. "Well, there's no easy way to say it. All of you soldiers who are awol will be reinstated without question. If you refuse you will be killed immediately. The United States government has records of everyone awol and will come soon to retrieve you. Every allied nation across the globe has records of all United States citizens, and they all have freely given these records to the U.S.. All soldiers will be picked up by Naval Ships, and military aircraft, and returned to the United States." "So..., these tour vehicles were always for this?" Mercedes asked with one eyebrow raised with her head tilted toward Jeff. Kevin didn't say anything as Jeff declared, "Our company is a coverup. I take it there are similar companies across the globe with these type of vehicles being used with awol military units. At least with our allies." Jeff released a big exhale as he finished talking. Then there was silence again. Kevin gained his composure and informed them of everything. When this talk came to a close, Mercedes and Jeff looked more like soldiers than pilots. It was as if a switch turned on within them. There minds already processed the information and embraced what was to come without conflict. The thought of rebuilding the United States actually pleased them. They didn't waste anytime checking in on the website Kevin provided.

On this website, United States citizens from all over the world could checkin to return. There were catagories for every essential position. After the military cleared a particular city, engineers and construction workers would rebuild, repair, or replace the cities infrastructure. Hotels would be used for housing. Firemen, policemen, doctors, nurses, and all city workers would be on standby. We found out farmers, and all of their land, were protected in secret. Farmers continued growing crops after the collapse and this is how the U.S. made money. Businesses which left were asked to return and would pay no federal taxes for five years. There would be no central banking system anymore. Money would be created by the United States without interest rates to any financial company public or private. The gold standard will be reinstated for this new currency. The Constitution will continue to be the foundation of our country. Bruce stood outside the closed door and heard some of the conversation. He walked in without knocking, "So when were you going to tell the rest of us about this?" "I was about to call you all inside, but you beat me to it." Kevin replied. He called all employees to his office over the intercom. He told everyone the truth. This is when Chad confessed about their unscheduled tour to New York. Everyone was grateful they didn't risk their lives and the lives of their customers.

As everyone shared their feelings and concerns, Kevin's office phone rang. Everyone hushed as he answered. His body language and energy shifted as everyone watched him. When the call ended, he shared the news. "Well team, we are officially out of business effective immediately as a tour company. Now we are a military combat unit..." Kevin stopped as Chad, Bruce, and Tiffany's laughter embraced his attention. "...What's funny?" Kevin questioned with a straight face. All three of them talked over each other with laughter continuing. "...Listen up Three Stooges. Our tour vehicles are actually retrofitted with military weapons." Jeff detailed aiding Kevin from the laughter. "If you all would have just looked inside your first aid kits you would know this already." Jeff stated as the laughter stopped on the word "retrofitted." Kevin continued giving the fresh information and instructions to his employees. There would be no more laughter as the tone of the situation settled on everyone. As Kevin talked with his office door completely opened, several United States military personnel entered. Everyone knew they were coming after Kevin's phone call. Everyone was briefed, updated, and instructed. Refunds were sent out to all remaining tours scheduled. The next day was training day with military personnel monitoring. Everyone left that evening with mixed feelings. The tour business was very lucrative and most customers returned monthly with new customers. Everyone decided to head to a nearby lounge to talk over drinks.

Everyone was down as they sat together in the booth near a big window. A server arrived quickly taking everyone's order. Chad, Bruce, Kevin, and Jeff, ordered beers. Tiffany ordered a pineapple margarita and Mercedes ordered a long island iced tea. Kevin thanked everyone for their service. Then he opened up and shared his funniest moments at work with them. Everyone began sharing their funniest moments. Server returns with their drinks. They all laughed together as they gave their food orders. They continued laughing and sharing as their food arrived. More drinks were ordered by everyone as the laughs continued. They were making the most of their company ending. No one was in a rush to leave and soon the stage area was opened for karaoke. Mercedes trotted to the microphone to go first. She started singing, "Hit Me With Your Best Shot" by Pat Benatar. The crowd warmed up and some started dancing as Mercedes entertained. Jeff visibly displayed he enjoyment seeing her singing. He rose up and walked over to the stage clapping. As she vocalized, "Hit Me With Your Best Shot," Jeff acted as if he had guns and shot his shot at Mercedes. Her smile brightened and she laughed over her words as she looked at Jeff shooting his best shot at her. As her song came to a close, the crowd clapped and cheered as she left the stage. She hugged Jeff and he gladly wrapped his arms around her as they rocked side to side laughing. At their table, everyone clapped along with the crowd. Jeff takes the stage and starts singing, "The Warrior" by Scandal. The crowd almost exploded hearing the beginning guitar intro. Jeff tried to sing the "Oh" lyrics at the start. The laughter resonated through the lounge. Mercedes danced in front of Jeff smiling as he entertained the crowd. Mercedes now shot her invisible guns at Jeff on the "bang bang" lyric. Kevin made his way to the stage seeing that the two of them were interested in each other. Tiffany joined them at the front of the stage. Jeff laughed so hard looking at the three of them, he could barely sing. He called them to the stage and they sung the ending of the song with him. When Jeff sang the victory is mine lyric, Mercedes wrapped her left arm around Jeff. The crowd was standing, clapping, and singing along. The energy was high in the lounge and when the song ended, the cheers were like they were at a concert. Kevin and Tiffany walked off the stage first, and as Kevin took Mercedes by her hand to help her off the stage, she kissed his lips gently and pulled back. They stared at each other for a few seconds as they crowd yelled, "KISS! KISS! KISS!..." They kissed and the crowd went wild. This tender passionate kiss lasted about ten seconds. As they exited the stage, another group took the stage ready to sing.

As they returned to their table, Chad and Bruce were gone. No one saw them leave. Maybe they went to the Men's washroom. They ordered a few more drinks and started eating their remaining food. Tiffany laid her head on Kevin's shoulder which caught Jeff's attention. Mercedes turned to Jeff expressing the same energy Tiffany was giving Kevin. "So Kevin, how long have you and Tiffany been together?" Jeff asked as Kevin smiled. "It's been two years." Kevin answered. "Jeff, you and Mercedes, be happy. Keep everyone out of your business. Love each other. Enjoy each other. Remember, keep everyone out of your relationship. You two will be just fine if you do this. Tiffany agreed with Kevin and they shared a tender kiss of their own.

Jeff needed to use the Men's washroom and Kevin joined him. This was a good time outside of work which rarely happened. Jeff was pleased to hear Tiffany and Kevin were together. He never suspected anything between them and this shows how good their character was at work. There was never any flirting or seeing them in his office looking suspicious. Jeff was happy for Kevin and Tiffany. Seeing Kevin assist with him having a good moment with Mercedes touched Jeff's heart. It was a good feeling seeing a man who was pleased in his relationship desiring to see another man get with a good woman. No one talked in the Men's room. As they returned to their table, Tiffany and Mercedes were laughing. Kevin asked, "What are you two laughing at?" Tiffany and Mercedes both explained their laughter which caused Kevin and Jeff to laugh as well. They continued sharing laughter until a military person walked up to their table. The laughter stopped as everyone seated witnessed the serious look on her face. She accompanied two men earlier inside Kevin's office.

Kevin asked her to have a seat, she declined. "Can you all please come with me?" Everyone followed her except Jeff who remained to leave $400 in cash with their server. The server was very pleased to receive a $75 tip.

As Jeff joined them outside, she introduced herself, "I'm Army 4 Star General Christina Daniels. You saw me earlier tonight. I'll get right to it. We have a situation..." As General Daniels took the time to explain the situation, several armed soldiers surrounded them as she talked. She had a folder which she placed in Kevin's hand. As he opened the folder, we gathered around him to see the contents. She explained the pictures we were viewing. Eagle 12 was destroyed and burning on the ground somewhere in New York City. We couldn't believe our eyes. We were completely lost and confused as to what happened. We viewed around twenty photos before General Daniels showed us the video of what happened. Kevin questioned, "How did you get a video?" "All of your tour vehicles have hidden cameras and video links connected to our military computer database. "Huh?... Wait... So you're saying..." "...Yes Jeff, I'm saying we have been watching you all since you launched this business." Stated General Daniels. As we started watching, we all clearly saw Chuck and Porsche operating Eagle 12. They departed the airport with a full tour of customers. General Daniels showed us video footage at the airport just before departure. Chuck and Porsche called the customers they had as regulars, and they paid them under the table. They reinstated the unauthorized NYC tour Chad and Bruce scheduled, changing it to this evening. "So, when we left work at 4pm, they went to the airport..." "...Exactly Kevin. While you all had a good time together, they took twenty people to NYC." "Wait a minute. They were supposed to be with us. We were having such a great time, no one asked why they didn't show up." Jeff shared as he tried to understand why Chuck and Porsche would do such a thing. "Can you forward the video to the incident please?" Tiffany asked as she grabbed Kevin's hand to hold. We all watched it together. They didn't use their drones for surveillance of any areas. They were having a great time with their customers. Suddenly they were hit with a rocket and took plenty of hits from bullets. They never had the defense system activated. The radar would have picked up the rocket so they could use evasive maneuvers. They were hit with another rocket that took out an engine making it spin. "How many cameras captured these final moments?" "That doesn't matter Kevin." General Daniels proclaimed without emotion. Several customers ejected, but were instantly killed by the blades. Seven customers parachuted to the ground safely as Chuck managed to steady the tour vehicle from spinning violently, but another rocket hit them. This time they had no controls. The tour vehicle went straight down taking lots of gun fire. The remaining customers ejected, but were hit with bullets. We could see their lifeless bodies parachuting to the ground. Chuck and Porsche survived the impact. Seconds later another rocket hit them. They both died instantly. We were so shocked the cameras continued recording after the crash and damage to the vehicle.

"General Daniels, can you replay the last 20 seconds in slow motion, I thought I saw something." Jeff asked. As the video played in slow motion, it appearred Porsche grabbed her mobile phone. Suddenly the tablet pinged, "Incoming New Video." She pressed play. Bruce and Chad were taking fire in NYC in an empty tour vehicle. They used their evasive maneuvers, but they weren't trying to get away. We all understood immediately they were hoping to rescue Chuck and Porsche. Porsche called them on her mobile phone and this is why they departed the lounge. They kept circling and avoiding fire, but they were trying to get to the wreckage to search for survivors. "Why didn't they fakt check? ...Why didn't they fakt check?" Mercedes questioned, but no one answered. "They should have told us!" Mercedes shouted. SuperNova had them surrounded and shot 5 rockets from a full three sixty angle. We saw them freeze up in surprise. "DROP DOWN!

DROP DOWN!" Jeff yelled. Instead, they went up allowing 2 rockets to hit them. They went in a spin as a third rocket hit them making a big hole on the right side. 10 rockets were launched again from a three sixty angle. There was a very big explosion before the tour vehicle crashed to the ground. No one made it. The customers who parachuted didn't do so to safety. The men were shot and killed immediately. The women were all dressed nice and smelling good, well, they wasted no time abusing them. It was caught on camera. General Daniels turned it off. "I'm very sorry about your friends and coworkers. I wanted you to know. Our company is not responsible. We were out of business when two of our former employees decided to have a rogue tour without our knowledge. We're in the clear. Once again, I'm very sorry." General Daniels and the armed soldiers with her entered a military truck, leaving us standing there near the front of the lounge. I thought it was very nice of General Daniels to include herself as part of our tour company family. I took this as her way of expressing that she actually cared for our friends. It seemed so genuine to me. "Kevin, she cares about us." Jeff said to Kevin as he nodded and smiled, "I thought that was very nice too. She had no emotion until she talked about our tour company. I'm glad she cares."

Our wonderful evening ended on a very bad note. Four of our pilots and friends are gone. Some of our favorite customers are also gone. Although we wished we knew beforehand, we thoroughly understood there was nothing we could have done to save our friends. At least Chad and Bruce tried to help, however, it was embarassing knowing they had weapons aboard they didn't even access. If they used their weapons, they would have probably lived and maybe saved the survivors. As we stood there outside of the lounge, General Daniels truck drove over to us. She lowered her window saying, "Do not go to NYC. Let me show you why." She let us see her tablet. The United States had now issued a no fly zone over the country. Everyone without authorization will be shot down without warning.

Military drones were launched to find and destroy SuperNova in NYC. "See you all at training in the morning." General Daniels released her words with compassion. Then they drove off into the night. We watched her vehicle until Tiffany started crying. Kevin hugged her as Mercedes tears began falling. I embraced her as I noticed the lounge was now closing. Everyone was exiting and heading to their cars. A few people stopped to say, "Hey! I loved you two tonight! Great job up there! Have a good night!" Everyone who greeted us were still full of the high energy we once had earlier this evening. Our ladies cried in our arms as the crowd thinned and we were left alone in front of the closed lounge. My eyes welled up as I noticed the familiar military truck approaching us. As she parked across the street from us, she lowered her window in the drivers seat. The soldiers were not present with her this time. "Soldiers, come here please?" General Daniels asked very politely. The ladies took a moment to get themselves together before the four of us walked across the empty street.

As we arrived at her lowered window, she smiled at us as we fixed our eyes on her. "I knew you all were still out here." She smiled again as we looked at her. "I really feel like I know you all. I appreciate the character each of you possess. I feel so bad we lost members of our family." We didn't understand her words. We looked at each other in ways which made her laugh in a good way. "Ohhhh, you don't understand why I'm talking to you in this way." She started laughing again. "Why are you talking to us like this?" Tiffany released feeling anxious to hear the General's answer. "I told you earlier that we have been watching you from the beginning. The truth is..., I have been watching you from the start of our company. I'm the one who recommended you, Tiffany and Mercedes, for his job. You too Jeff. I did the same for Chuck, Bruce, Chad, and Porsche. Kevin, you were handpicked to be the manager. We made you believe there were other candidates. It was always you alone. I have companies all over the world with United States soldiers employed. The President of the

United States has a very soft heart for all of you. The no fly order was issued to protect you and the rest of your team from anymore casualties. We are ready to restart our country. Thanks to Memory Lane Tours, and other businesses I started across the globe, we have generated enough money to begin the rebuilding process." "What do you mean? How?" Kevin questioned. "Kevin, all of Memory Lane Tours profits went one hundred percent to the United States Government. The United States has had income from farming as well. We are still feeding the world in secret. It's been fifteen years since our country ended, so the world believed, but we will be respected globally again. We will be even better than before. This time we will be tougher on crime. So much so everyone will be terrified to be a criminal. Did you think Memory Lane Tours was a private company? Not at all." She paused talking for a moment. We just looked at her processing everything she's said up to this point. "It's ok. You'll understand everything after our training tomorrow. It's ok Kevin - Jeff - Tiffany

- Mercedes. (She smiled again) One last thought I want to give you before I leave you guys tonight. You've thought about me many times, however, you could never quite put your finger on me. Get some rest guys. 'By all means, Keep Up the great work. GCD.'" She drove off as Kevin's eyes were enlightened with pure revelation. Kevin says with sincere astonishment, "Everyone..., our emails... always ended ...with the signature, 'By all means, Keep Up the great work. GCD' GCD means General Christina Daniels. She is our owner. She personally hired each other us. This was always a military operation. Oh my gosh!" The same astonishment which captivated Kevin, engulfed the minds of Tiffany, Mercedes, and Jeff, with the revelation they never truly went awol from the United States Military.

- The Subway -

STORY FOUR

* * * *

The sound of the approaching train increased as it pushed air toward us in route to our station. I loved looking in the distance seeing the lights shine in the dim lighting of our subway as the air blew upon me. I enjoyed this feeling. No, I loved this feeling. The air blowing my clothing like I'm in Michael Jackson's "Bad" video. Most of all, I love trains. However, my friend Carlos despised my love of trains. I hated when I bumped into him on my way to work. On this day, he was not present and I recorded my favorite train, Run 076, as it entered our station. I always rode in the front rail car with the train operator. She was very beautiful and many of us were trying to figure out what race she was. She had a look as if she was White, Black, and Latina. Her eyes were slanted like she was Asian. She never talked to any of us. Her only words were "All aboard." "Good morning." and "Have a nice day/night." When our train arrived at the last stop, Giza Terminal, she always stayed aboard until we were all off of her train. She really kept to herself. I appreciated my forty two minute train ride everyday and was disappointed when she wasn't operating our train. No one handled 076 like her. She always gave us a very smooth ride. No jerking or hard breaking. This never happened. One day when I exited her train at our last stop, she looked at her phone and smiled. She looked up as I was walking by. Her smile shined as bright as the whites of her slanted eyes. From this day, I called her Daisy because of the bright whiteness of her smile.

As I exited the train station, I saw Carlos standing on the bus stop. I couldn't believe he was actually early today. "Look who's running late today. It's Pierre the scientist." Carlos shared acting very flamboyant in his colorful business suit. "Ok, Ok. You beat me here, but I'm not late. How's your commute Mr. Train Hater?" "Oh shut up. It was going quite well until I missed my bus. I was trying to get to work a little early today. I believe I'm close to a breakthrough with our new prenatal medicine. I might stay late depending on todays results. How is your work going?" Carlos detailed to Pierre before asking his question. "Well, our research is now completed. We will go through the results again and submit it to be tested today. So, what are y'all going to name your prenatal med?" "I'm not sure of the name just yet. Yes, here comes our bus. Ummm, I want it to have a happy name since it's to help eliminate birth defects in high risk pregnancies." "Why not see if you could name it after your sister? After all, she's your motivation." That's a very good idea Pierre, thanks." Both of them rode the crowded bus to work in silence. As soon as they exited the bus, they continued their conversation. "You should submit the name idea as soon as possible before someone else names it Carlos." Pierre suggested. "It's up to you Carlos. I believe this would be an amazing legacy for your family." Carlos showed several emotions varying from excitement to nervousness. "Are you doubting this Carlos?" Pierre asked wondering how Carlos would respond. "Well, I'm a bit hesitant to ask. What if they say no? That would really hurt me." Carlos admitted as he dropped his head down and stopped walking. "But what if they say yes?" Pierre stated as he pushed Carlos on the shoulder making his body sway back. Carlos nodded and looked up nodding, "You're right. The story behind this medication would be a big deal. Thanks Pierre. I apprecite you." "You're welcome bro." They started walking again. "Hey Pierre, what is the project your department is working on again? I'm sorry I can't remember it." Carlos asked. "We are working on a medicine for dogs. In simple terms we are trying to prevent dogs from going blind from certain illnesses common among them. Our grant for this research was a life saver and I'm pleased with our hard work. I'm looking forward to seeing dog lovers smile knowing their pet will not go blind." They arrived at work as they talked. The company they worked for owned a huge skyscraper downtown. The two of them greeted everyone in passing. As they waited for the elevator, several jokes were said by their coworkers. This was a good place for researchers and scientists. Izzy Pharmaceuticals had a great code of ethics everyone was actually happy to read. Pierre and Carlos worked on different floors, and had different lunch schedules. Most days they only saw each other in the morning.

Pierre had a great day. His work had wonderful results and was verified by other resarechers. Everyone in his department went home excited for dog owners. After leaving the building, he saw his bus and ran to it smiling seeing the bus driver was clearly waiting for him to board. Pierre thanked the driver and eased his way through the crowded bus. He sent a text message to Jillian his nerdy ex-girlfriend. They agreed to breakup because they couldn't spend quality time together. Both of them had careers they loved and would never make time for each other. Work was priority for both of them, and he wasn't surprised when she didn't respond.

As he departed the bus, he went to eat in a small restaurant inside the Giza Egyptian Museum across the street from the Giza Terminal. Pierre dined here a few times a week and knew several employees who seated him at his favorite table; if it was available. After ordering his meal, he watched a news report revealing a new discovery by the pyramids. Without asking anyone, one of the employees turned the sound up on the big flatscreen tv, and turned the music off playing throughout the restaurant. "...exciting. We couldn't believe it's preserved in such great condition with no cracks. We cannot figure out why this is not broken in a many pieces. 'Please tell us the details of the Obelisk?' Of course, so far we can read about half of the Egyptian Hieroglyphics on one side. We are actively excavating it, and we believe if we continue to work around the clock, maybe in a day we will see exactly how long it is, and read all of the hieroglyphics. The Egyptian government has decided to restore this Obelisk. They are sending for some major equipment to lift it up and place it where it was originally. We cannot wait to see it in its glory." Someone walked over speaking in her ear live during the interview. "Oh wooowwwwwww!!!!! The hieroglyphics are perfectly clear on one side. I'm about to go see it for myself. Nice talking with you." The employee turned the sound off and restored the restaurant music. Pierre's meal was placed in front of him about the same time. He had some time before his favorite train departed. He knew the schedule by heart. He ate his food in peace alone, left a nice tip, and went into the subway.

His favorite train entered the station from the new section of track just finished under new construction. The public transportation company was in the process of explanding the subway to go further into the city and beyond into the distant suburbs. The thing Pierre appreciated the most were the new long stretches of straight tracks so the train could go even faster. These new trains only reached speeds of 40 to 50 miles per hour because the stations were close together, and because there were just too many curves causing the train operators to slow down for safety reasons. 076 was standing outside the station before it entered. Pierre took pictures and a few selfies with the train behind him.

After the train entered the station, a man exited the train and Daisy walked out of an employee section to prepare the train for service. As he approached me, I asked him, "Good evening. Why was the train just standing there?" The switchman replied, "I was staging the train. Well, I was waiting until it was time to bring the train to the operator." "Do you know when the new tracks will be opened?" I asked smiling anticipating a start date. "Tomorrow. As a matter of fact, here's a schedule. It's the last one I have. You should take a look at our website for more information. Have a nice day." "Thank you. You have a nice day too." I responded as the doors of 076 opened for service. I gladly boarded and enjoyed the ride until I exited on Jackson Blvd and waved at Daisy who said, "Have a good night." I was happy. No, I was very happy. Today was a good day. I stood still and watched 076 depart Jackson, and walked home to my spacious condo.

Little did I know, Carlos had a terrible day at work. The test results for the prenatal medication were inconclusive. All the numbers and data left him frustrated. He had several arguments with his team and this was very unusual. He left work and returned with a big bag. The building was almost empty except for a few researchers staying late working. His department was empty. No one seen him, but he was captured on surveillance. Inside his big bag was a cage he had to put together, along with two small mice which were pregnant. He put the cage together and added the pregnant mice. Our company did not allow animal testing, but tonight Carlos was going to test his prenatal medication on the mice. This was a very bad idea. His judgment was visibly clouded by his emotions toward his sister who was born with major birth defects. She died seven months after being born. Carlos was nine years old when this happened and this sparked him to become a research scientist to prevent birth defects. He gave each of the mice his experimental prenatal medication. This was a decision he would regret. The mice should have been thoroughly examined before given this medication. Carlos didn't have any data to measure or the right equipment to record the results. What was he thinking? What happened to him? Were these mice previously having babies with defects? We didn't know or understand his reasoning for doing this. Obviously, I know this because I saw the footage. I only wish I could have talked to him prior to this myself, but it was too late by the time I saw this video.

While Carlos was destroying his career and life's work, I was in my abode after having a great day. I took a hot shower and relaxed. I looked at the train schedule the switchmen gave me. I couldn't believe my eyes when I saw 076 would be the first train to depart on the new tracks northbound to the new stations. It was an evening scheduled departure just after the p.m. rush hour.

This was to avoid crowds if something went wrong. It would be the first time these trains will move at top speed. No curves, no turns, and no slow zones of any kind. The transit company used older trains with no computer or digital systems to test these tracks. I couldn't wait to move at top speed. Now we would officially have our own high speed train system like many other countries across the globe. Our trains were proclaimed to be faster and I couldn't wait to see if this was actually true. You know what? Even if it wasn't true, I didn't care. I just wanted to go fast with Ms. Daisy on the train controls. "Please let Daisy be the operator. This would be absolutely perfect." I said to myself with great anticipation. I played my favorite music by Johann Sebastian Bach and opened my large patio doors to see the skyline from my tenth floor view. A sweet cool breeze entered as usual with the lake being nearby. I poured a glass of wine to end my night as I relaxed on my sectional gazing at the view until I feel asleep.

The next morning my mobile phone disturbed

my good nights rest. It was our job demanding I come in immediately. "We have a situation! We need you here now!" I rushed to work ahead of my normal routine and schedule. When I arrived at work, I was met in the lobby by our company CEO, "It's Carlos. I'll show you what happened on video." There was a small office in the lobby we used for miscellaneous things. "Watch this Pierre!" Our company CEO declared with horror in her face. "Krystal, what is it I'm about to watch?" "Just watch it! You'll understand." Krystal declared again. I watched Carlos break our code of ethics and violate our corporate social responsibility policy, but this wasn't the worse part. After administering the prenatal medicine, the mice began shaking violently. It looked like one of them died at first, as the other mouse kept shaking. The second of the two finally stopped. The look on Carlos's face was disappointment. He started crying, but suddenly looked up when one of the mice began growing. There must have been a sound with the growth that triggered him to look up. Our video had no sound. Within ten minutes this mouse looked like a rat. It was still pregnant, but bigger. The other mouse didn't grow or move at all. The bigger mouse walked over to the now smaller mouse and began smelling its belly. Then it quickly moved to the other end of the cage. The belly of the smaller mouse started shaking and began to swell although the size of the mouse didn't grow like the other mouse. Carlos had a recorder taking voice notes for data purposes. The belly continued to expand until it burst. The babies of this mouse were bigger than it's mother. There were five babies which didn't look like they were pups. They looked like adult mice. All five began eating their mother's dead body. When Carlos witnessed this he tried to remove the other mouse to avoid her becoming a meal. The mice who were dining on their mother's remains all stopped when the covering was opened. Looking up at Carlos, they all looked very aggressive causing him to close the cover. He looked very nervous as if he didn't know what to do next. As he looked around and pondered on his next move, he jumped back. The pregnant mouse began growing again. She was visibly bigger and continued to grow slowly, but evenly before his eyes. The sound of her body growing was very evident now. She was now much bigger than the five mice finishing up with their mother's body.

The five mice looked at each other with aggression for a few seconds and started fighting. As the fight intensified, one mouse was injured and squealed in agony causing the other mice to stop fighting. In an instant, the four mice devoured the injured mouse while it was still alive. Carlos knowing this was a horrific result panicked. He looked around trying to figure out what to do. We could see sweat beading down his face. The squeaking mouse sounds turned into loud painful squeals as his siblings torn them apart alive. We knew this because Carlos covered his ears as his jaw dropped to the floor. He looked around the laboratory with his hands on his ears. His eyes were stretched as sweat dripped off his chin. Carlos trotted away and returned with a cart. He put the cage on the cart, and placed a medical equipment cover on it from the supply room. He exited his department and left the building with the cart.

I immediately dropped my head knowing this was not going to end well for Carlos. "Well, what is our next move Pierre?" Krystal asked looking disturbed. "Ok, ok, we need to send a team to his residence. He stays a few blocks from me. Maybe he took the subway home. If he took the subway, maybe they would let us see the footage in the stations and the footage on the train. Send the team to his apartment now, and call the transit company afterwards." "Pierre, I trust you. I was in the process of promoting you prior to this situation. Just so you know." Krystal admitted just before sending a hazmat team to Carlos residence. "Come on Krystal, let's head to the train station. You can call the company on our way." Pierre suggested strongly as they prepared to exit Izzy Pharmaceuticals.

The transit company was hesitant to allow us to

see the video footage until they understood the potential bio hazard that could occur. Inside the Giza Terminal, we met the manager who called the upper level managers concerning ths situation. We had to thoroughly explain the entire situation to get them to allow us to see the footage. This took almost forty minutes. Just before we were allowed to see their video footage, the team called Krystal saying Carlos didn't answer the door. She stepped away from the transit manager and told the team to break into Carlos's apartment. She waited on the phone until a complete search was documented. "Carlos is not here. There's no sign of the cart." I was in midsentence when Krystal interrupted, "... Carlos never made it to his apartment. Can we please confirm he never entered the subway? This would help us both out. If those mice..." "...Stop! Ok!" The upper level manager shouted over the speaker phone. "I'm sending the footage now from the time he left Izzy. It's unedited. Call me back if he was on our property." He hung up as we gathered around the terminal managers computer.

We watched the video together. There were four separate angles. We normally entered from the north side of the terminal across the street from the Giza Egyptian Museum. "We should have seen him by now. It's doesn't take this long unless the bus driver didn't allow him on the bus. Or just maybe, he went somewhere else." I uttered as we were all focused on the computer screen. "Where else would he go? Nothing makes sense." Krystal asked as I saw something. "Wait! Rewind it!" I shouted. Mr. Everett, the terminal manager, replied, "Ok! You don't have to yell!" "Sorry Mr. Everett." I apologized. "Look, right there. There's his reflection on the glass. It's Carlos, but he's not going into the subway. He's across the street walking south very fast. He still has the cart." I explained as I was pondering on why is he walking pass the terminal instead of entering. "Mr. Everett, I think he walked to your next train station. I believe he entered the New York Avenue Station." I suggested knowing it was just a hunch of mine. Mr. Everett made the call to his superior and he sent the video footage from the New York Station. Six minutes later, we saw Carlos enter the station. He looked very stressed and nervous. "He's trying to avoid us tracking him." Krystal shared as we watched the video. He took the elevator down to the subway still sweating heavily. We watched him closely taking notes of everything. He boarded a southbound train run number 142. He was in the last car marked B642. Mr. Everett called his superior manager updating him. I noticed instantly Carlos didn't disembark at Jackson. "Why didn't he get off? His apartment is a few blocks away. I'm trying to figure out what he is doing. Where is he going? Krystal, call the team and have them head to the next train station. He didn't go home. Maybe he's still in the subway." "Good idea Pierre." Krystal replied as she walked away to make the call. "Pierre, I hope Carlos doesn't do anything crazy." Mr. Everett expressed sounding very concerned. "If these mice are growing, or whatever it is you told me, if they get out of the cage. Well, you know what I'm saying." "Mr. Everett, I don't want to even consider the thought." "Well, you need to. What's the plan if they get out?" The terminal manager asked, but I didn't respond. We both watched Carlos ride the train with the cart still covered.

After riding four stations passed Jackson, he suddenly covered both of his ears on the video. "Oh no! No! No! No!" I shouted triggering Krystal to hurry back to the computer to see the video. "Oh no is right." She said softly. Mr. Everett inhaled deeply before saying, "I know this is bad news. Are you going to share it?" "Well sir, Carlos covering his ears means the pregnant mouse is growing again, or the other mice are eating another sibling. Hmmm..., and..., it could also mean both. At least that's what it meant on the footage we have at Izzy's." The terminal manager dropped his head and picked up his phone. "Sir, I believe we have a E-27 situation..." His upper level manager called the police and fire departments to have them on standby. Mr. Everett, along with Krystal and myself, took the time to update the police and fire department heads of the situation.

Carlos finally stood up and pushed the cart to the train door. It was eleven stations passed Jackson. "Why did Carlos get off the train at Lois Blvd?" I muttered being completely baffled. The upper level manager was on speaker phone. He directed the police and fire department to Lois. Carlos waited for the people who exited the train to leave the station. As they were going up the escalator, a northbound train entered the Lois station. After those people boarded the train, the station platform was empty. Carlos started pushing the cart into an employee only section. He opened the gate which didn't have a lock, and walked into the unauthorized area. We could all see the tail lights of the northbound train that just left Lois. Between Lois, and the next station Cypress, was a supply area that had several big concrete storage blocks. As the next northbound train approached, Carlos hid behind the storage blocks as the train passed. Mr. Everett stated, "Carlos has a good hiding area. The train operators will not see him." Mr. Everett's phone started ringing. He answered,

"Wait, what? Where? Copy!" He rolled his head around his shoulders in a circle, then sighed, "Well, that call said we have an emergency in the same exact area we are watching on video. The information giving to me conveyed the train made contact with something. The police and fire departments were already in route. I'm hoping for the best possible outcome. Let's see what happens."

We forwarded the footage. Carlos stayed in this area for a long time. After a train passed him, he lifted the cage up off the cart. We witnessed Carlos struggling to lift the cage. We knew this meant those mice were growing and much bigger. He placed the cage on the edge of the catwalk. He jumped down to the tracks and carefully lifted the cage placing it in the middle of the tracks. He left the cage covered. We all knew at this point what Carlos was doing. At least we thought we knew. This section of track had very dim lighting and the train speed was fifty miles per hour. Carlos stood on the tracks crying. I shook my head believing the emergency already in progress was Carlos and his mice ran over by a train. I couldn't believe my eyes when Carlos laid down in the middle of the tracks in front of the cage. "Please stop the video. I don't want to see him die. I believe we know what happens next. Krystal, call the police and see if they need our hazmat team to recover the remains of the mice." Krystal made the call, but Mr. Everett kept playing the video. He even forwarded it to get to the incident. Pierre saw he was still watching the video and walked out of his office. Krystal followed Pierre as she finished her call. "Ok, the hazmat team is in route to the incident. Hopefully, there's no serious damage to the train. We are being held responsible for the major delay that's underway. The subway is closed down pending the investigation. We do not need to be on the scene. They are documenting everything and will update us shortly. Ok..., what's wrong?" "I asked Mr. Everett to stop the video, but he's still watching it..." "Pierre! That's his job! There is an active emergency connected to our company and research. Calm down." After inhaling and holding it for several seconds, Pierre responded, "You're right. I'm just hurt my friend is dead. Why couldn't he talk to me before he made this decision? What happened to him? I just wanna know." I teared up thinking about our fun times. "COME HERE!" Screamed Mr. Everett. "LOOK AT THIS!" We hurried to his computer. He rewinded it as we approached his desk. "Ok. Watch this closely." He asked as our attention focused on the screen. We watched the video together. Carlos was laying vertically between the tracks. The train was in the distance, but approaching at fifty miles per hour. The air was being pushed as usual. The covering on the cage was moving and this meant nothing to me. However, Mr. Everett detailed as he paused the video, "Look, you see that? The cover is moving toward the direction of the train instead of blowing away. The air from the train would not make the cover move toward the train. Now watch this." He started the video again, but slowed it down. The cover moved up for a moment and went back down. Carlos covered his ears as he laid between the tracks. The cover rose up again toward Carlos. A shadow emerged toward Carlos as the cover started blowing away from the approaching train. The shadow covered Carlos's right shoulder as he jerked away disappearing from view as the train passed over him and the cage.

After the train exited the video, there was what looked like blood and scattered remains in the area. Nothing looked like human remains. The train stopped in the distance about three thousand feet away. "I hate to say this, but Carlos could have Been dragged or picked up by the train. His remains could be in front of the train, or there could be pieces of him under the train consist." Mr. Everett expressed with empathy trying not to offend or hurt Krystal and Pierre. "How long until the subway opens back up?" Pierre asked seeing it was now almost lunch time. "It can take up to four hours today since this is not a regular emergency. We have to clean up all remains and disinfect the entire stretch of subway track. We also have to clean the undercarriage of the train. There could be body parts logged into wheels..." "...Ok! We got it!" Pierre shouted at Mr. Everett for being too graphic. "I do apologize. I've been on this job for almost thirty years. It's sad to say, but I'm kinda use to this. We here on this job have to get counseling from time to time because we have lost our sensitivity to families. I do apologize." Mr. Everett stood up and walked out to get some air. We stood there several seconds before Krystal suggested, "Well, I suppose we can leave now. I'll be heading back to Izzy. Why don't you take the day off? I'll see you tomorrow at work. Get some rest. Clear your mind. I'll do the same after I talk with the police and fire department." "Are you sure you don't need me there? I'd rather help you to be honest. I don't want to go home." Pierre expressed in a sincere manner. "Ok, let's get back to Izzy." She said as the two of them exited the terminal and caught a cab.

After Pierre assisted Krystal with the police and fire department, he went into his locker to grab his journals. He had several which he covered in large plastic Ziploc bags. After someone spilled a beverage on his journal years ago, he learned to protect his words which was his heart written in pages. He had a big backpack he kept at work with his journals inside. He never took his journals home. He loved writing on his lunch and on his breaks at work. However, Pierre believed he needed to take his journals home to write concerning Carlos. Now that he was alone in the locker room, he sobbed over his friend. He released it all without shame. Krystal heard his cries which triggered her tears. Everyone hearing his weeping also cried and went to the lockers. Twenty seven coworkers cried with Pierre over the death of Carlos. They hugged and embraced each other in tears. Izzy employees looked at each other as family. This was a major blow to this company.

After the tears subsided, a carrier arrived leaving a certified letter signed by the receptionist. Krystal was called over the intercom to collect the letter. Pierre walked with her since he was leaving the building. They shared no words on the elevator and were quiet as they walked toward the receptionist. Krystal opened the letter and erupted into tears. Pierre embraced her. She cried in his chest very hard for several minutes. No one witnessing this said anything. It had been a long day for everyone. When she pulled away from Pierre, his white business shirt was soaked with her tears. "I'm sorry about your shirt Pierre. Here, read this." Krystal disclosed as she placed the letter in his hand. After reading it, Pierre dropped his head understanding why Krystal wailed. "After clinical trials with pregnant women who were pregnant with a child with defects prior to birth, our tests conclude each mother gave birth to healthy baby boys and girls. Twenty thousand pregnant women participated and twenty thousand all had healthy births. We monitored these babies over the first two years of their lives and they are all still healthy. We are going to recommend this drug be named after Carlos Sanchez's sister who passed of birth defects. He suggested her name, 'Merry,' which was her nickname because she was a happy baby, but we will also use her legal name, "Miracle." The name brand will be Merry and the cheaper versions, which will be made in the years to come, will be named Miracle. Truly, this drug is a miracle. The next several pages have the data from our findings. Great work Izzy Pharmaceuticals. Your contribuation to humanity will bless families all over the world....." I handed Krystal the letter and walked out of the building.

I was walking toward Giza Terminal. I wasn't in a rush. So much was on my mind. If Carlos just waited one more day. This thought made me return to Izzy. I went to his department and asked everyone, "What were you arguing over yesterday?" Nine people heard my question. Only one person dropped their head. I asked them directly, "Jenny, what happened with Carlos?" "Well...," "SHUT UP JENNY! Jonathan screamed. I called security on my company radio. "Continue Jenny." I asked as security arrived. "Hold Jonathan security." They grabbed him tightly as Jenny continued, "Well, Jonathan told Carlos his drug would never work..." Krystal walked in as Jenny shared what happened yesterday. "...and that he's wasting his time. This made Carlos very angry. Jonathan started laughing and this..." "Lead Carlos to do what he did today. Thank you Jenny. Jonathan you're fired. Get him out of the building." Krystal boldly proclaimed as she logged into a nearby computer disabling Jonathan's security clearance and company identification cards. Krystal called the police and informed the captain of Jenny's testimony. The police department provided Jenny with a security detail due to Jonathan's threats as he left the building. After comforting Jenny, I left work and started walking toward the Giza Terminal again.

My news alert sounded on my mobile phone. I read, "The Subway is finally reopened after a track level emergency earlier in the day. The new stations, along with the new tracks, will open per the schedule this evening." This brought a smile to my face. I literally had twenty two minutes before run 076 departed Giza Terminal Northbound. Then I thought, "Wow, Giza will no longer be the last stop on this route anymore." I grabbed a cab and arrived at Giza Terminal in ten minutes. I was still smiling which was a very big deal for me. I gladly entered the Terminal, but stopped to see there were workers present changing the signs from Terminal to Station. I took a few pictures and selfies with the new signs being installed, then hustled into the subway. I had three minutes to departure and couldn't wait. As I stood on the platform, the train was being brought into the station from the underground train yard. The train looked as if they just washed it in a car wash. It was shining and dirt free. I heard the employee door open and Daisy exited on her way to operate 076. This caused me to smile even bigger. In spite of the bad day, I now had a smile on my face. "Good evening." I saluted Daisy. She responded, "Good evening to you. I'm very excited to see how fast we can go. Are you excited?" Daisy asked me as I smiled even bigger. "Yes I am excited. I've been looking forward to this experience." I replied. "Me too. All aboard." She added as she opened the doors of the train. A local news crew entered the station to capture 076 departure on the new tracks. They started recording us seconds after arriving. They recorded us sitting on the train and recorded Daisy preparing the train for service. The cameraman was moving around very fast capturing footage. The news reporter had thirty seconds to talk before we departed. "This is Sharon Jones. On the scene here at what's now Giza Station. Run 076 is getting ready to depart northbound to the new station Park Avenue, that is ten miles away. This train will only take about two minutes to arrive. Let's watch 076 depart." The cameraman turned around as the door alarm sounded. Daisy said in the microphone, "All aboard Riders. Doors are closing. All aboard." She never uttered those words before with so much enthusiasm before. The doors closed. The train thrusted out of the Giza Station. The train was practically empty because the subway had recently reopened. I didn't care. I was the only rider in the front car. As we picked up speed, there was not a bump of any kind. It was like we were floating through the air. I loved it! I heard Daisy shout, "Whew!!! Yes!!!" This brought joy to my heart knowing she loved this experience too. I started recorded us through a small section of window in the direction we were going. Wow!

"Jimmy make sure you record 076 until we can't see them anymore. Ok?" "Ok Sharon." Jimmy recorded 076 which kept increasing speed in a straight line. Jimmy was leaning over the tracks recording 076 when a large flash of glowing blue light reflected in his camera. Sharon watched Jimmy as he recorded 076 in route to Park Ave. She glanced to her left seeing a couple holding hands on the far end of the platform. She turned to Jimmy who was still recording when a strong breeze pushed upon them causing their clothes to blow a little. Sharon thought it was the next train. She leaned over the tracks, just to the left of Jimmy, and looked for a train, but there wasn't a train. She stepped away from the platforms edge and looked throughout the station seeing no one. Jimmy was still recording 076 with the glowing blue light radiating in his camera. After this light stopped illuminating, the train was no longer in sight. He walked over to Sharon who asked, "Did you get it?" Jimmy answered, "Yes. I got it. We can go." They departed the empty station.

Krystal's mobile phone started ringing as she sat in her office. It was Mr. Everett. "Good evening. The subway has reopened. The investigation took a lot longer than usual because, well, we never found Carlos's body." "Wait, huh? How? I don't understand." "There was no body. We searched the entire section of track and Carlos was not found. The cage was destroyed on impact. The blood on the tracks was mice blood, and they had very big bodies. The mice remains will be arriving to Izzy soon. Your team gathered the remains. Like I said, we didn't find Carlos's body. We are going to look at the video footage again. Maybe we missed something. I'll update you when I get more information." He hung up as Krystal sat in her chair puzzled and trying to make sense of Mr. Everett's words. She called Pierre's mobile phone. It went straight to voicemail. She waited a few minutes and called him again. This time she left a message, "Pierre. This is Krystal. Please call me. It's very important." She ended the call.

Mr. Everett looked at the footage again. This was the closest camera angle facing southbound in the direction the train followed. Once the train passed this camera, there was no way to see the impact in front of the train. This time he logged into a different camera south of Carlos, and the cage, recording northbound. From this angle he would clearly see the impact of the southbound train although the footage was further away. As he waited for the footage to download, he read over the operators statement from the emergency. "The operator stated. It looked like something moved before he made contact with the cage. Operator says he didn't see a human." Mr. Everett watched the video footage from the trains front camera. It looked like something moved just like the operator stated. He slowed it down frame by frame. It was only a blurr in each frame. "Beep." The video was finished downloading. From this angle, the blurr was visible in like manner, except the blurr came toward the camera. This made Mr. Everett watch the front camera train footage again. This time he let it play further frame by frame. The blurr moved out of the way of the train, and moved on the catwalk headed southbound toward the camera facing northbound. Mr. Everett called upper level management. "We have another situation. We need to send this footage to the police to be analyzed. I think the pregnant mouse survived and the remains were from the other mice that were eating each other. Maybe she killed them because she was bigger. If this is her, we need to find her before she has those babies."

The police arrived in record time. They brought portable equipment for video analysis. After uploading each video, the results only took a few minutes. The footage was now crystal clear in real time. The mother mouse picked up Carlos and ran with him. We all sat there in silence. No one said anything for a few minutes. The mouse was almost as big as Carlos. She out grew the cage just before the train hit it, and probably killed the other mice. "Why did she save Carlos? Was she his pet? This would make sense." A detective suggested. "Maybe he took care of her, and she remembered his care. So she saved his life." Mr. Everett contemplated. Let's call Krystal and update her.

"Hello, this is Krystal." "Krystal, this is Mr. Everett. The police are here with me. They sent a video analysis unit to clarify our footage. Here's the police chief." "Hi Krystal. Like he told you earlier, we didn't find Carlos's body. After cleaning up the blurry video footage, the pregnant mouse saved Carlos before the train ran over the cage. We are very curious about Carlos and this mouse. Did he have this mouse as a pet? This would explain why the mouse saved his life. Would you have any information concerning this?" Asked Police Chief Grant. "I have no idea if he had a pet mouse. Standby, I'll ask my team who was at his apartment earlier today. Please hold." Minutes went by as Police Chief Grant was on hold. "Hello. I'm back. I'm emailing our footage of Carlos's apartment to Mr. Everett's email. Ok, you should have it in a moment." Mr. Everett checked his email confirming he received it. He in turn sent the video to the police equipment connected to his computer. After viewing the footage, there was a container that looked like flour, but it was Kruse's Perfection Mouse and Rat Food. There was also another cage. Maybe she was, or rather is, his pet." Krystal expressed, but not really understanding what was taking place.

After the police explained everything to Krystal, she updated her team at Izzy. "The violent mice who ate each other are dead. We will examine their remains and do a full blood analysis. The pregnant mouse, who kept growing, is still alive and saved Carlos's life. By the way, she's almost the same size as Carlos. We need to find this mouse before she have her babies. The pregnant mouse was Carlos's pet. The police believe this is why she saved his life.

She picked him up off the tracks and ran him to safety. This is a strong fast mouse. She'll probably be faster after having her babies. Maybe Carlos is safe somewhere with her. However, her babies will not know Carlos and his life may be in jeopordy with them. This goes for all of us, especially if they are violent." Mr. Everett heard Krystal end her update and added, "We are about to monitor all subway cameras live, so we can find..." His radio received this transmission as he talked, "...076, what's your location? 076 are you monitoring your radio? 076 please respond..." "Excuse me Krystal. Here's the police chief." As Krystal and Grant talked about the mouse and Carlos, Mr. Everett used his job radio, "This is Triple 4, 076 report your location immediately. 076, call in your location." Mr. Everett sent an email to the manager assigned at the new station after Park Avenue. Mrs. Johnson responded to the email and went downstairs to the Michigan Station. 076 was scheduled to arrived to two minutes. She had her radio with her and when 076 did not arrive, she asked on the radio, "076, report your location. 076 do you hear me? Respond 076." Mr. Everett was monitoring his radio and responded, "This is Triple 4. 076 respond to your managers. Triple 4 to Triple 5." "Triple 5 your message." "Triple 5, do you see 076?" "Triple 5 to Triple 4, I do not see 076." "All units. All units. Does anyone see 076? Find 076. This is priority." About seven minutes later, "Triple 5 to Triple 4. Run 228 just arrived at Michigan Station. No sign of 076." "Triple 4 to Triple 5, thanks for the update."

As the 228 entered Michigan Station, the smell of smoke filled the air. You could hear lots of thuds as the train slowed down with black smoke oozing from underneath the train. Triple 5 couldn't believe her eyes. In all the years she has worked on this job, she has never seen a train look this bad on brand new tracks. Just before the train completely stopped, the train was rocking side to side as the thuds were now even louder. "Triple 5 to all units, we are closing down the subway effective immediately. Run 228 just entered the Michigan

Station with black smoke and it sounds like all of the wheels are flat in the rear. The train is swaying. Send track inspectors immediately." (A southbound train arrived on the other side of the station. This would have been the first train southbound to enter this section of track. This operator made announcements saying the subway was now closed and gave travel instructions to their riders.) The train operator of Run 228, Michael Bibbs, opened the doors after he berthed his train in the station. He had a head injury with blood running down both sides of his face. Triple 5 asked him, "What happened?" Michael's head was outside of the trains window as he finally opened the doors. He didn't address Triple 5. He made this announcement, "Attention riders. I do apologize for the rough ride. I'm injured. I'll be checking this entire train to make sure you all are ok. We have a manager already here on the platform who will call for medical assistance if you need it." After his announcement no one exited the opened doors. He was hoping someone walked out unharmed. He exited the motorcab, walked into the passenger area of his front rail car, and saw several riders on the floor. He walked as if he was dizzy stumbling somewhat. Triple 5 walked into the train talking on her radio, "This is Triple 5 at Michigan Station on the northbound platform. I'm requesting medical assistance for the train operator. He has a head injury with blood and appears to be losing consciousness." She grabbed him by his arm and sat him down. "Michael, I'll check your train. Sit here until help arrives." He nodded his head as his eyes rolled back. He leaned to his left side and slowly plopped down on a passenger seat. Mrs. Johnson checked the entire train making multiple radio transmissions updating the situation. As she arrived in the seventh rail car, the smoke was very black and small flames were rising up from track level. This was the case for the last three remaining cars as well. "Triple 5 Northbound at Michigan. I am requesting the power be removed. We have a F-72. I repeat, we have an F-72. Cut the power northbound at Michigan." Seconds later she heard the train motors stop, signaling the power was removed, and the flames died down until they were gone. The fire department arrived and treated Michael. They rushed him to the hospital. There was a total of ninety seven people on this train and all of them were taken to the local hospital with serious injuries. Fortunately, no one was dead, but each rail car had blood from the injuries of the riders.

Meanwhile, Krystal called Pierre, "'This is Pierre. Sorry I can't take your call. Please leave a message. Thanks.' Pierre, this is Krystal. Please return my call. This is serious. Thanks." What is going on tonight? Krystal asked her team. Pierre and his train are missing. There's a big mouse in the subway who is Carlos's pet. What on earth is going on? She called Mr. Everett, "So, the train is missing and we have to find a big mouse in the subway. What is our next move?" Krystal asked feeling defeated. Mr. Everett was also feeling defeated, but tried to be positive, "Krystal, it's been a long day. Let's all try to get some rest, and we will get back at this tomorrow. Ok?" "Ok. Have a good night Mr. Everett." "You too Krystal." Phone call ended. Mr. Everett didn't inform Krystal of the latest events. He knew he wasn't going to get any rest at all, but he wanted her to get some rest. Mr. Everett drove his car to the Michigan subway station to assist Mrs. Johnson. He brought the company laptop to download the video footage on Run 228. "I'm glad you're here Travis, Mr. Everett's first name, I can't believe what happened tonight. It makes no sense at all. Look at the damage to this train. What are your thoughts? What do you think happened here tonight?" "Gloria, Mrs. Johnson's first name, I really don't know, but I'm hoping this is not the mouse and her babies doing. I'm already shocked 076 is missing. I don't know what to think of this just yet. Did the inspectors arrive yet?" "I don't think so. They haven't called in on the radio." After Travis downloaded the videos from the trains harddrive, he emailed them to upper level management. Then they both walked the entire train consist at track level to see the damage under the carriage. Each of the wheels were cracked and some were missing pieces of the wheels. Each of them used their flashlights as they walked by each individual rail car at track level. As they arrived to the last three rail cars, their mouths dropped in disbelief. Gloria didn't notice this on the platform with there being so much smoke and riders needing medical assistance. The doors of the last three train cars were lower than the platform. She thought the trains suspension systems were offline. "Travis, how is this possible?" She asked shaking her head. "Gloria, we need to walk into the subway..." "...No! Let's call this in first! Request for the police..." "Ok, ok, you're right. We need someone with weapons just in case this mouse did this. You're right." Both of them returned to the platform. He requested police assistance to walk the tracks. As they waited for the police, the track inspectors arrived and didn't want to wait for the police. As they headed toward the stairs leading to the tracks, the police entered the platform. The track inspectors didn't get far. They were entirely stunned with what they found. Gloria, Travis, and the police joined the track inspectors who were gazing in total bewilderment. The police shared the same reaction. One of the police officers expressed their thoughts, "How on earth did this happen? This is practically a new train and the tracks are brand new. I'm..., I mean..., oh my goodness." Gloria voiced, "This is unbelievably not normal. Let's walk." Gloria pulled out her company mobile phone and began recording. All eight police officers had their guns extended with their flashlights. Gloria, Travis, and the three train inspectors followed the police. After walking three hundred feet southbound on the northbound tracks, the police suddenly stopped. Travis questioned, "Officers, how come you stopped walking?" "Come and see." Uttered one of the police officers. The police were two by two in a row of four. Each of them moved aside so the transit managers could walk inbetween them to the front. No one said a word. The silence was very loud as everyone could hear each other breathing.

Travis broke the silence, "The train tracks are gone. Why? I mean, how...," Gloria talked over him, "...This is not happening." The tracks were all gone. This explained why the wheels on the train were so heavily damaged. "We need to see the surveillance footage. This will be the only way we know what exactly happened." Travis articulated calmly as they all started walking again. "Gloria, when we checked Run 228s train, there were tracks inside the station. The last three rail cars were not on the tracks. It was like it derailed. This section of tracks have no switches, no intersections, no junctions, or signals. So we know this train didn't run a signal, split a switch, or go too fast on a curve to derail. What if this train somehow ran over the mouse causing the last three rail cars to derail?" "This doesn't explain why the tracks are now gone. We need to see the video. Let's not try to figure this out without the video. Let's just document everything and compare it with the video." Gloria comprehensively released as they all continued documenting the subway.

After walking the entire length of the subway from Michigan to Giza, they called in their findings causing upper level managers to join them in the subway. It was now very late into the night. High ranking police arrived on the scene. The high ranking police officers and the upper level managers decided to watch the video footage of 228. Everything was smooth until the train was preparing to arrive at Michigan. The train jerked vehemently just before entering Michigan. This is when Michael received his head injury. The train was fast enough to drag the last three cars into the station, although the tracks disappeared from underneath the last three train cars, as it was slowing down to stop inside the station. The last three cars dropped to the concrete ground without tracks causing smoke, and flames. This is why the wheels are not on the tracks inside the station. Everyone took turns watching the footage until the sun was rising. The police commissioner contacted all of the local news media and set up a press conference at the transit company for eight in the morning.

At eight o'clock a.m. the press conference began with the transit CEO. "Morning everyone. On last night, we opened our new stations and new tracks. Our first departure, Run 076, departed on time, but did not arrive at the next station Park Avenue. (Gloria just realized what she missed during the subway inspection a few hours ago. There was no Park Avenue station. Her eyes were so big as she looked at Travis standing next to her. She whispered the news in Travis's ear. His eyes were now just as big as hers.) There were twelve people aboard this train and we are currently going through video surveillance trying to understand what happened to 076. Here's what our video cameras recorded. (The video footage began playing on a very big screen inside the transit companies press room.) Ok, as you see, 076 is moving very fast. Our cameras are approximately one city block apart. In this frame you see 076 passing this camera, and then our cameras stopped working. There's nothing captured. As you keep watching, the cameras start working again, but 076 is gone. This has us baffled and we need everyone's help trying to figure out this mystery we have on hand. This is all we have currently. Any questions?" "WAIT! WE HAVE FOOTAGE!" A reported yelled as she and a man made their way to the front of the press room. "I'm Sharon Jones and this is my cameraman Jimmy Chong. We were on the scene and Jimmy recorded the train as it departed until it was out of sight. This footage was never edited or shared with our audience in any fashion. Give us a second to set it up for you." She revealed as Jimmy began setting up the video. Everyone was gathering closely when Jimmy declared, "The video is ready." The transit CEO asked everyone to be quiet down, then asked Jimmy, "We are ready. Thank you so much. Maybe this will help us figure out this mystery. Press play." The video brought many people to tears seeing Daisy, Renita Hedgewood, preparing her train for service. She was well respected by everyone at the transit company. As the train departed, everyone's eyes were laser focused on the screen. The large flash of glowing blue light reflected is what raised everyone's eyebrows. After the light disappeared, the train was no longer in sight. "Please let us have a copy of this video Jimmy." The CEO asked as he continued, "What is causing this flashing blue light?" The CEO eyes were still on the screen when he saw something. "Jimmy, rewind the video please?" He asked with a curious kind of look on his face. Jimmy rewinded the video and played it again. When Jimmy was in the act of moving his camera away from the view of the train no longer in sight, the tracks had a glowing blue light on them for a second it appeared. It could have been longer if the camera stayed on the line of sight with the tracks. "I am very pleased we have this new footage. Thank you so much Jimmy and Sharon. This has given us a starting point to research. There will be no more questions at this time. We will update you as soon as we have analyzed this new footage with the police. Until further notice, our subway service is suspended until we understand what's going on.

We do not desire to have anyone else disappear in like manner. We will have more bus service available. The subway bus service will only stop at the stations the trains would normally stop at. Hopefully this will help make up for the subway closure. Thank you." Krystal watched the press conference from Izzy. She understood exactly what was going on. The transit company used 076 as the only reason to close the subway while they look for the pregnant mouse and Carlos. At Izzy, our hearts were hurting over Carlos and Pierre. We were trying hard to press our way through this situation although we were all very sad.

At Izzy, all of us were talking when we noticed the Giza Egyptian Museum on the news. Someone turned up the sound, "On a brighter note, we have better news coming from our beloved local Giza Museum president who's live in Egypt with our corespondent Jean." "Thanks Sheila. I'm Jean Martinez here with Rebecca Harmony the president of the Giza Egyptian Museum. Please tell everyone about what we are about to see." Rebecca smiled as she began to say, "As you already know, the Egyptian government restored the Obelisk found in front of the unfinished temple. The unfinished temple in front of the Sphinx has been a mystery for us to solve and we believe this Obelisk may have some answers for us. There are hieroglyphics on two sides of the Obelisk. After studying the sayings on each side, we believe the hieroglyphics were to face the rising of the sun and the setting of the sun. This Obelisk is huge! It's precisely 36 meters in height. One side reads, 'Ra provided our protector.' The other side reads, 'Beware of our protector.' We do not understand these sayings, but as we continue to excavate, we hope to find more history laying in the sand. We are about to show the great reveal. The countdown has begun." "Ok everyone. They are about to remove the giant tarp blocking our vision in 5, 4, 3, 2, 1." The tarp was removed. Cheers filled the air from those attending the reveal. The Obelisk looks brand new. Sheila asked Jean, "Jean, it looks like they just made it today. How is it so well preserved?" Jean asked Rebecca. She responded, "We are not sure just yet why it's so preserved. To be honest with you, it appears as if they never raised it. With it being in front of the unfinished temple, maybe it was abandoned. We are uncertain in the moment. However, we believe there is more to be discovered here in this dig. We will keep you all posted." "Back to you Sheila." Jean happily said as the camera showed the Obelisk before going back to Sheila in the studio, "In other news, there's a missing couple last seen yesterday. Maybe they were on train 076..." Sound was lowered and everyone dispersed to their departments.

It was a long morning for everyone. The hospital reported all the passengers on Run 228 will be just fine. However, Michael was still unconscious from his head wound. He lost a good amount of blood, but they had his blood type on hand. They are expecting him to recover. The police were busy with the families of the passengers. Most of which came with attorneys to the hospital, and all are ready to sue the transit company. The transit company was scratching their heads in disbelief over all three of these situations. Right when they were about to go to lunch, here comes more families with attorneys to sue the transit company over their vanished family members. It was absolutely chaotic.

Mr. Everett had his hands full when he stepped out abruptly. He went to the breakroom to relax from the stress of the day. As he walked into the breakroom, the only employee was exiting as he entered. The television was already on. This was the only noise he heard. He went to get his lunch from his locker. He placed his homecooked meal in the microwave, and got a beverage from one of the vending machines. After retrieving his drink, he walked toward the television to turn it off. He just wanted peace and quiet. He grabbed the remote control when Gloria walked in, "Travis, there you are. I was looking for you." He took a deep breath. "Oh I'm sorry, am I disturbing you?" She asked tenderly. He took another deep breath, "It's been a very long, long morning. I just wanted some peace…" "…The sun is setting here in Egypt and we are hoping the sayings on the Obelisk will reveal something…" "…I talked to Krystal today. She told me Pierre was following this Obelisk story." Gloria shared now that the story caught her attention. They both remained quiet as they watched the special news segment. "…Ok everyone. We are standing here in front of the Obelisk. As you can see, we are facing the Sphinx, and the pyramids of Giza. I'll be quiet as we watch it together." A very beautiful sunset was in progress in Egypt. There was not a cloud in the sky. As the sun inched its way closer to touching the horizon of the Earth, the soft gentle rays of the sun shined on the Obelisk. This caused beams of light to shine forth from the top. There was an Egyptian symbol at the very top no one had ever seen before in Egyptian history. It is a smiling woman with bright white slanted eyes riding a snake with eleven people. We believe it's Hatshepsut who was the Great Royal Wife of Pharaoh Thutmose II of the Eighteenth Dynasty. There's no name written with the symbol. As we all stared at the beams of light, we noticed they moved upon the ground toward the three big pyramids. As the sun went down, the beams went up. No one has ever witnessed anything like this in the history of Egyptian Archeology. Some of us were thinking it was going to show us the location of secret tombs, or treasures we have yet to discover. Or maybe it would show us the figure of the Egyptian god Ra or an image of Hatshepsut herself.

"Listen, I really don't want to watch this Gloria." Travis stated as he went to the microwave to get his lunch. As he walked toward the microwave, Gloria screamed, "OH MY GOD!!! LOOK!!! LOOK TRAVIS!!! LOOK!!!" Travis turned around and couldn't believe his eyes. The bright white beams of light was on each of the three big pryamids 076. 0 on the left, 7 on the middle, and 6 on the right. The sphinx had a bright beam of light on it's mouth. The light looked like a big smile upon the sphinx lips. Rebecca Harmony began to talk with passion, love, and astonishment, "This is beyond mind blowing. History is being made live on media outlets all over the world. I can't believe what we are witnessing. In my city and hometown, as a matter of fact, yesterday. It happened yesterday. A train disappeared with those numbers. 076 disappeared. It vanished. I'm in awe. I'm about to open my laptop to look at the image on the top of this Obelisk, and a picture of the train 076 with the operator. Look at these images together. Could this symbol be of Renita Hedgewood? They look just alike. I can't say I believe in time travel, but maybe some how, some way, it happened. We had no reason to think of any person outside of known Egyptian history to try to idenify this symbol." She turned her laptop toward the camera. "Look. Could it be this snake represents 076? It's not a snake, but a train. The train disappeared with 12 people in total. There are 12 people in total on this snake. I'm not saying this is 076, but 076 is beaming on the Giza pyramids before our eyes. WAIT!!!!! OH MY GOD!!!!!... WHAT... IF... THE... TRAIN... IS... HERE?!!!!!

(To Be Continued In Volume 2)

- DIN -

STORY FIVE

* * * * *

"As of May 2024, Voyager 1 was 162.7 astronomical units from Earth. Over 15 billion miles away. It's power supply is declining. It's power is expected to stop collecting scientific data very soon. It takes 22.5 hours to receive a radio signal from Voyager 1. Approximately 28 hours ago, we received data from Voyager 1 informing us it has detected sound waves which are not from Earth. The photos associated with these sound waves only display stars. We believe there could be a planet with intelligent life such as our own, and we sent instructions for Voyager 1 to change course to the direction of these sound waves." The room erupted with various people from news networks across the globe asking questions. George looked around the room from his small platform, appearing to be unbothered as his eyes slowly went to a female reporter from DSN (Deep Space News). DSN was a news network mostly unknown by popular culture. George respected this network and desired it to receive greater recognition. George pointed to Sarah, "Are you sure this data is correct? Is there any chance it's a malfunction being that Voyager 1 is losing power?" Sarah questioned with a stern face moving her blond hair away from her right eye. George Jones paused for a moment causing other reporters to start asking more questions. He lifted both his hands signaling to wait while he processed his thoughts. "... We are fact checking our data aggressively. I honestly have mixed feelings. On one hand I hope it's a malfunction. However, if it is sound waves from intelligent life, this would be exciting to know we are not alone in the universe. Unfortunately, we've seen lots of sci-fi movies with violent alien life. If this is alien life, we hope it's not the worst-case scenerio. We will keep you guys updated. No further questions at this time." In an instant, he walked away entering a nearby door heading back to his office.

His landline phone was already ringing as he entered the door. "Hello. Yes. Ok. Yes. Understood. I will take care of this right now." He hung up the phone and logged into his computer. A knock jarred him for a second. Deep breath in, he held it, released, "Come in." Five members of his team rushed inside with new data. "George, you have to take a look at this!" Lisa kindly exclaimed as George continued typing on his computer trying to email the previous data to other space agencies across the globe. "George!!! LOOK AT THIS!!!" "OK LISA! DAMN!" He grabbed the paperwork out of her hands, visibly frustrated as his team gathered around his desk as Lisa continued, "We just received this from Voyager 1. There's a new signal. As you can see, Voyager 1 communicated with the sender of this signal and gave them directions to Earth. Keep reading. I'll know when you see it...." "Oh... my... gosh..." "You read it. The sender of this signal not only confirmed if the directions were correct, they confirmed it 64 times.

Soon thereafter, Voyager 1 detected the new sound wave very distinct from the first. This waves coordinants are directed to Earth..." "...Wait, ..." "Yes, you can read..." A team member steps in, "That's not necessary Lisa. Let George continue." "Thanks Frank." George addressed Frank appreciating him for always trying to keep everyone respectful toward each other. George proceded to say slowly while thinking, "What happened with Voyager 1? It detected this new transmission... (The other 3 team members looked extremely nervous as George thought out loud. Lisa's body language showing, 'get to the point, time is ticking.') ...the sound wave is moving toward earth, but according to this data, it didn't move pass Voyager 1. It's not travelling in different directions or spread out like the first wave. It's direct. They are aiming it to us. This is odd... Ok..., Voyager 1 sends us this data. Why did Voyager 1 communicate with them? How did Voyager 1 communicate with them?" George paused after his question. Lisa boldly adds, "The sound wave will arrive to Earth in approximately sixty four hours. For some reason this new sound wave is moving slower than the speed of sound unlike the first wave. We need to tell the world..." "... Don't float your boat just yet Lisa. Give me a second..." George released pondering on what to do next. Frank raised his hand, "I have a suggestion. (George nodded expressing 'let's hear it.') Since this new sound wave is moving slowly toward earth, let's ask Voyager 1 how did it communicate with them. Let's see if Voyager 1 interpreted the sound waves. Let's try to determine what was shared. We have just enough time to send and receive a message." The office was silent for a moment. Even Lisa didn't respond which was a victory to the team members. George asked, "Does everyone agree with Frank? I agree. (Everyone nodded.) Are there anymore ideas? (Everyone was silent.) Ok. Frank, do it!" The team members were leaving as George told Lisa to stay and close the door behind her, "Lisa, let me show you the email I was about to send." Lisa read it over silently. Her stern exterior eased displaying she was pleased with the message. "Now, just add our new data to this email and that should do it George." Lisa stated as her body language showed she looked very concerned. George was silent as he added the new data to the email. Lisa looked nervous and started fidgeting which caused George to notice. "What's really on your mind Lisa? Don't hold anything back from me." "George, I really have a bad feeling about this. Maybe it is all the alien invasion movies I've seen." "Well Lisa, at least we won in the movies." George shared as he started laughing. Lisa smirked at him as he continued laughing. Her face changed into a semi-perfect smile. "Ok Lisa, check out this email." Lisa looked it over and declared, "It's perfect. Good job. Well, I look forward to hearing what our colleagues will say. It surely appears we are not alone. I hope the sound we receive is peaceful." "Me too." As George stood up, "Let's join Frank and be focused on what we need to do. We need your resting bitch face now." He laughed so hard as Lisa joined with his laughter. This was an inside joke they shared between the two of them.

George and Lisa enter the observatory. They had a nice distance to walk to get to their team members. As they gathered, Frank hung up the phone appearing dismayed. Everyone was quiet for a moment. Each team member looking over and around each other. No one desired to ask Frank the question which was written over all of their faces. Frank sighed as he placed both of his hands on his head. His elbows clearly needed lotion. It was evident his elbows were rubbing on his desk from stress all day. George broke the silence, "Frank, what is it? Focus your thoughts..., and tell us." Frank inhaled, exhaled loudly, "I sent the instructions to Voyager 1. As soon as I sent those instructions, moments later, we received new data from Voyager 1. We just went over this data and I had to call the Office of Space Affairs...." "...Why didn't you inform me first Frank?" What did you say to them?" Frank inhaled again as he lifted his head up and folded his hands together on the table. "The data we received from Voyager 1 shows a planet. It looks a lot like ours; only bigger. Here, look at these pictures." Lisa stood by George as they viewed the pictures together. After observing each of them, they were both shaking their heads in disbelief. George replied befuddled at the data, "This cannot be right. This planet looks exactly like ours. Maybe this data is corrupted because of the power supply depleting. Maybe Voyager 1 sent us pictures of our own planet after we launched it back in the 70s. Did you compare these pictures to our records?" "Yes George. We are confused too." Frank expressed. "Ok team. Let's review the data we first received..." As George instructed his team, Anthony, a team member who doesn't say much, but when he adds to any conversation or discussion, he normally shocks everyone with his meticulous communication. Anthony walked over to one of the deep space telescopes. He heard George as he continued instructing. Anthony directed the telescope to Voyager 1. As the telescope positioned itself to the new coordinates, Anthony walked back over to the team. "... so everyone. Comb through the data again, afterwards, we will compare it. Ok?" Everyone said ok as they all dispursed to complete their assignments.

"...Shut the hell up! Everyday all of you talk loud and laugh at dirty jokes! I'm filing another grievance! Maybe the union, which I hate, will actually do something I actually approve of which is shutting all of y'all the hell up in this breakroom!" "Why do you keep coming in here if you hate us so much? Go eat your lunch in your car, and stay away from us..." Glenn loved silence. He hated noise. It didn't matter who or where the noise came from. It all started when he was a little boy. Glenn was exposed to arguing, fighting, and disputes within his own family. Every day his family fought over everything. He soon hated his family after many years of hearing traumatic sounds. His ears became sensitive to any noise many years later. He despised hearing lawn mowers, construction workers, and all everyday noises from the city. At some point he hated leaving his home. He was very traumatized by his childhood unlike his brother George. George engulfed himself in his telescope and didn't care about all the fighting in their home. Glenn and George weren't very close. Glenn was into various sports so he could be away from home. George didn't care about sports. He only cared about everything in outer space. Glenn and George both receives college scholarships. Glenn's was athletic and George's was academic. Glenn failed his astronomy class. This caused him to lose his football scholarship. He wanted to attend a summer class to make it up, but once he found out he lost his scholarship, he quit school and gave up on football. His parents were very hard on him and once they yelled at him, he simply left their home and never returned. After his parents called local police, Glenn contacted the police saying he ran away. He didn't desire his information given to his family, and since he was an adult, the police honored his choice.

"...Why are you still working here Glenn? Don't you have a concert to sing at?" Everyone in the breakroom erupted into strong laughter. The coworker started singing, "We've only just begun, the romance is not over..." The entire breakroom started singing with him. This caused Glenn to exit the breakroom vocalizing his irritation, "I hate you dumb bastards! My vacation can't come quick enough! He slams the door. The breakroom coworkers had a conversation concerning Glenn. "It works every time. Just sing a Glenn Jones song and he will leave." "This dude is weird. He always complains about us talking." "What gets me is the fact he won the lotto and still works here, who does that?" "Oh yeah, he did win the lotto. How much was it?" "He won like 26 million dollars. Where is that money now? Who knows?..."

It was now one hour later and all assignments should have been completed. Each team member entered the observatory seconds apart. The only person who didn't look worried was Anthony. He gave his analysis first. "Everyone. As I went over the data, the only thing that was definitive are the sound waves themselves. I entered the original sound wave into Aitken (NASA super computer), and I was astonished when I received this answer." No one asked or said a word. Anthony announced, "Aitken deciphered this sound with no other possibilities, 'Is anyone there?'" "Give that to me Anthony." George stated as he reached out to receive the papers. Anthony continued, "Along with those words are more pictures from there world." Anthony had a folder nearby he handed to Lisa as George continued reading Aitkens analysis. "Are these the same pictures?" Lisa uttered as she opened the folder. Everyone started adding their two cents creating a small commotion. Lisa yelled, "EVERYONE COME LOOK!" The team gathered around her. "They look like us. Is this true? Can this be true?" Another commotion rose which was heated and no one stopped talking until the phone rang. Frank started walking toward the phone, George stopped him and incisted he answered the phone. Frank stopped looking disturbed. George picked up the landline. "...... ok. .... Yes sir. We have .... Yes sir." George was obviously bothered as he hung up. "Well, everyone was apparently monitoring your findings Anthony. NASA will share your findings with the other agencies. The landline rang again. George answered, but this time, he put it on speaker. "George Jones, this is Ron Jacobson from..." "...I know who you are, please get right to the point." "Ok George, our team has analyzed the data you sent us via email. We have pictures from their planet..." The team listened to Ron not grasping they would learn they missed essential information. Ron explained, "... There was a message which was hidden. Maybe they were testing our intelligence..." "A hidden message? What is it?" George asked while looking at his team who all looked mystified and anxious at the same time. Ron proclaimed, "The message says: 'Respond, and we will come.'" Everyone was silent, but you could see the wheels turning in everyone's face. "Hello... hello? ...Oh, so I see you didn't have this information. Well, I'm glad we found it. I'll let you guys discuss this further." Ron hangs up.

Anthony continued, "Everyone relax, settle down, close your mouths, it's ok. I was going to inform you of the hidden message. We were interrupted remember? We have to get our heads in the game. George, check your emails, maybe you received something that could help us." George logged into his account as the team went over the pictures. Each of them sharing how human they looked and how their planet looks so much like our own. Their structures and technology looked like our own. Lisa says breaking the stillness, "Should we be afraid? I mean, they look like us. Would we go to another planet if we received a signal? Ron said the data detailed, 'Respond and we will come.' Should we be concerned? Just think, they can't travel across the universe, right? If their technology is similiar to ours, maybe this sound wave coming will share something positive?" George interrupts Lisa, "... Ok team. Every space agency on Earth is examining this data. Now that we are focused, Anthony, is there anything else you had to tell us?"

"As a matter of fact, yes. Their message, 'Respond and we will come,' could mean many things. Maybe they will communicate with us via sound waves..." "Or?" Lisa asked looking a bit afraid. Maybe they will actually come to our planet..." "Is this possible Anthony? They look like us and their technology looks similar to ours. How can they travel 15 billion miles to our planet?" Anthony paused, and turned to everyone, "George, while you and Lisa were in your office, I asked Frank if I could send the message to Voyager 1. The message I sent was very clear, 'Target the planet sending the frequency and record everything, and send it back to us asap.' In addition, I asked one last request of Voyager 1. 'Scan the new sound wave and send the data to us asap.' We need to know and understand as much as we can about this race. So team, let's be brave as we do our jobs for this agency and for humanity." Everyone nodded and cleared their thoughts of all negativity. They had about forty hours before the data could be received from Voyager 1. Out of nowhere, George asked, "Where is Voyager 2? Is there any way we can direct Voyager 2 to scan the direction where Voyager 1 is postioned?" No one answered. Let me make a few calls. Hopefully it will only be one call. "You don't need to make any calls. You're quite frustrated presently. Voyager 2 is 12 billion miles away from earth, in the opposite direction, remember?" Anthony explained to sober George. Disconcerted and discouraged, George released a loud sigh as he drops his head down knowing he was not in the game. He started turning red, so much so that his scalp was red in the middle of his bald spot. "It's ok George? I believe we all understand the gravity of this situation. We're not judging you." Lisa uttered with compassion as she approached George giving him a warm embrace. George cried in her arms provoking the team to release their emotions. Frank hugged Jessica, who also started crying. Jessica was the fifth member of their team. She was a very quiet personality because she didn't speak the best english. She worked at a different ageny a year ago in Japan. Anthony did not show much emotion until the four other members of their team all hugged each other. Something about this moment touched Anthony as he joined his team in a group embrace. He let go of the weight of the world and released his tears. Little did they know, this was exactly what they needed to refocus themselves. They needed to see and analyze the obvious, and not think of the possibilities out of fear. We weren't alone in the universe and they relinquished the terror which clung to all of them.

The team worked round the clock and worked with other agencies across the globe. George took a break and called his parents. He shared everything with them. After all of these years, no one in their family has heard from Glenn. George was able to find him and acquire his mobile number, but didn't call him. Glenn had a video of him go viral because of his coworkers. They recorded themselves singing to Glenn in the breakroom. Glenn's reaction entertained the entire planet receiving over twenty million views in a week. George saw the video and noticed the name of the company in the background. He called this company and verified Glenn worked there. This company freely gave George his brother's information. George didn't want to risk Glenn changing his number so he never called. However, with the uncertainty of this situation, he decided to call Glenn after he talked with their parents. Glenn didn't answer. Seconds later, "Who is this?" lit up his phone via text message. "It's George your brother. Can you call me? Please?" No response. Five minutes passed by, and in the exact instant George was going to walk back inside his phone rang. "George, what do you want?" "Glenn, it's good to hear your voice again. I've missed you. We've all missed you." George shared feeling relieved. "George, what do you want?" Glenn repeated, but this time being more assertive. "Lil G, there's a sound wave on it's way to Earth as we speak. It will be here in approxiately 10 hours. We should be receiving informtion from Voyager 1 at any moment concerning this situation. This is definitely from an alien race. We are hoping for the best, but, well, you know the saying." "Preparing for the worse. I know. This sound wave, will it pass Earth or is it directed to Earth?" Glenn asked knowing he hates noise. "It's directed to Earth Glenn. So, I called to say I love you. Be safe." George hung up the phone wishing his brother told him He loved him. George entered the automatic revolving doors. As he walked through them his text messages sounded, "I love you too Big G." George smiled and shared this with their parents via text.

There was a major press conference scheduled to update the world. George was not feeling very confident he could handle the pressure. He asked Anthony to speak for their agency. George returned precisely when it began. The best minds across the planet addressed the world. They shared the pictures and the hidden message although they didn't say it was hidden. There was a plethora of questions and each one was answered carefully yet truthfully. George was on the side near the rear because he had nothing to say. This position made it easier for him to be snatched by the arm by Jessica who remained in the observatory. George immediately knew this was serious as Jessica rushed him to the observatory. "George, this is very important. You must see this." Jessica declared to George who picked up the pace to keep up with Jessica. Her long Asian hair bounced to the rhythm of her steps. George slipped in stride, but gathered himself without falling. His thoughts strongly disrupted his unconscious ability to job without thinking. Jessica grabbed his hand slowing the pace simultaneously. George's face showed a grateful smile as seconds later they entered the observatory.

After George caught his breath, Jessica had the data ready for George to examine. After fifteen seconds his eyebrows raised and mouth opened wide. "The pictures we first received were fake. They do not look like us and their planet is nothing like ours. They look hideous and their technology surpasses ours. Their cites and planet look over populated. Somehow they scanned Voyager 1 without Voyager identifying it. They examined

Voyagers data bank and used our pictures as their own. They created similar photos and transmitted them to Voyager 1 purposely. This was to make us be at peace. It was to decieive us, trick us, or possibly cause us to stop searching for their planet. When we changed Voyager 1s direction to their signals origin, this is when they sent false data, so we can receive it. However, Voyager 1 continued taking pictures and scanning their galaxy thanks to Anthony. Jessica, is this everything?"

Jessica looked down and inhaled as she looked up. She released her breath, saying, "No, that is not everything?" Her body language made George know something serious was coming. "George come. Look at the panel. What is missing?" George immediately recognized the importance of Jessica's question. "What happened to Voyager 1?" "Jessica responded looking very concerned, "I do not know the answer George." George rapidly went over the data himself when a transmission came through from Voyager 1. He stopped what he was doing. He didn't wait a second. He hurried to get the new data uploaded into Aitken. It only took seven minutes. George printed it out and hurried back to the observatory. He desired to read it with Jessica. They sat down together and went over Voyager 1s data. Voyager 1s last activity was scanning the new sound wave headed toward Earth. Voyager 1 scanned this wave a little over twelve minutes when another sound wave was released directly at Voyager 1. Voyager 1 recorded it and sent all findings to Earth. After sending the last transmission, Voyager 1 stopped transmitting. George straightway attempted to send Voyager 1 a message, but the link was disabled. He attempted to reestablish it, but nothing he did worked. George and Jessica began combing through the data again to see if something could explain this. Jessica suggested, "May be the battery finally died." George didn't respond as he looked through the data. He knew it was something worse. There was only one logical answer. "Voyager 1 has been destroyed. Even if the battery died, we can still track Voyager 1." The light should always be on.

George made a phone call for mainteance to replace the bulb on the panel. They came in record time, but the new light bulb did not illuminate. George dropped his head as the rest of the team entered. The press conference was over and Jessica wasted no time handing them the final data from Voyager 1.

Anthony walked over to the telescope with the farthest range without looking at the final data. He set the coordinates to Voyager 1 thinking he would be sending another message. As the team went over the final data, he was frustrated because he couldn't find Voyager 1. He didn't observe the indicator on the panel displaying "there was no link" to Voyager 1. "I.. I don't.. understand. Where is Voyager 1?" Anthony uttered in disbelief as the team walked over to him with the final data. "Voyager 1 is destroyed? This can't be!" Anthony was angry and hurt simultaneously. Anthony took the paperwork as Lisa shared, "So, what does this mean?... This race... knows... we know the truth now, huh?" Lisa sat down and placed her right hand on her forehead which partially rested on her sister locs. As she frowned in worry her pecan skin wrinkled as a few tears fell. As her tears increased she vented, "So... these monster looking creatures are on their way here, and Voyager 1 is gone. I suppose we shouldn't have launched it, huh?" "That remains to be seen..." George replied, but was interrupted by Lisa who stood up with makeup running down her face, "...They are coming! We are defenseless! Get that in your head! We just looked at their world! We have a 'before and after' pic seconds apart. How can one picture show a totally inhabited world and a second later it's empty? Did they attempt to hide themselves from us? How can they manipulate Voyager 1? I'm glad we know the truth, but what can we do with this information other than inform everyone? I am concerned about this soundwave..." Anthony interrupted Lisa, "...It's just a soundwave, how bad can it be? Maybe it's just communication..." "IT'S OBVIOUS TO ME IT'S MORE THAN JUST COMMUNICATION!!!!" After yelling Lisa leaves to get some fresh air.

Jessica pursued her.

"Frank, how much time do we have before the soundwave arrives?" Anthony asked trying to figure out what to do next. "We have three hours and thirty two minutes. Shall we call our families and go to our bunkers? What do we do now?" Frank asked with no confidence of hearing a cognitive answer. No one answered him. Anthony started sharing the information he failed to view with the team, "Here is what Voyager 1 discovered before it went offline. Here's what their planet really looks like and this how they really look. The absolute final piece of data we received from Voyager 1 is the shocker. I'm very confused. Aitken appears to be confused as well. According to Aitken, these pictures are from the same planet. This is how their planet really looks and this is how they really look, but moments later all of these images are gone. Maybe Lisa is right. They are trying to hide themselves. If this is true, their technology supercedes ours if they can hide. I'm grateful though." "What do you mean?" George asked as

Frank walked over. "I'm grateful they could not erase Voyager 1. Maybe they tried and it failed. Therefore they destroyed Voyager 1. How do you two feel about Lisa's feelings?" No one wanted to answer. As Anthony walked off, he adds, "Maybe it was a mistake to launch Voyager 1..., and 2." Anthony leaves the observatory. George and Frank sit down wondering what to do next.

George and Frank shared no words as fear rested upon them. The time was ticking and although they weren't talking, their minds were racing trying to figure out a plan. The unknown coupled with the pictures of reality tormented them. George formed beads of sweat as he pondered on the worse. Frank was rubbing his temples. When he's under pressure, he receives headaches which can cripple his day. He didn't forget his medication today and took his daily prn dosage. After talking his pills, Frank asked George, "What do you believe this soundwave really is? Will it be an invitation? A greeting? A warning?..." George didn't say anything. "...George are you going to say anything? We need you George." Frank walked over to a different computer and began typing. Seconds later the wall timer was activated. No one had to ask how much time before the soundwave reaches Earth. Frank walked over to George who was in his own world presently. He glanced at him for a moment or two, then he also exited the observatory.

Frank joined Jessica, Lisa, and Anthony outside. As soon as he arrived, he walked up to a conversation already in progress. "...Maybe you're right Jessica. It's just a soundwave. We have transmitted many soundwaves ourselves into deep space." Lisa said trying to embrace the peace of Jessica's words. "Thank you Jessica." Lisa added as she turned toward Anthony as he nodded in agreement, "It's a soundwave. We are going to hear a transmission from another world." He started smiling. Frank started smiling seeing his team working to having the best possible attitude in this situation. The four of them talked another twenty minutes until they were all laughing together.

If only George was outside with his team. While his team encouraged each other, he was stressed out. He made his way to the landline and made a phone call. He was patched into another call already in progress. As George listened to this conference call concerning the soundwave, his stress levels increased. Sadly, this call was full of negative possibilities. Every nation across the globe readied their military forces. Each leader addressed their nation asking everyone to take this seriously and take every precaution to insure their safety. The last transmissions from Voyager 1 caused firey exchanges among the leaders. Some debated the battery died and others declared it was purposely destroyed. This was the only thing they did not agree on. The team returned to the observatory and found George soaked in sweat with a grimace on his face. "George, are you ok?" "NO! I'M NOT OK!" He reacted. "George, you need to calm down. Look at us. We're good. It's ok how ever this plays out. We are not alone in the universe and it's ok. However it plays out, it's ok. Ok? We all talked about it and have come to the conclusion that we can't change anything, so why stress about it." Anthony took George by the arm suggesting he stands up. George rose up and Anthony walked him outside for fresh air. As they were walking out, George started crying as Jessica, Lisa, and Frank concentrated on the conference call on speaker. As they listened, they all knew why George was breaking down mentally. The world leaders were preparing for an invasion and this caused them to look at each other as if they shouldn't have a positive or nonchalant mindset.

Once again, Glenn Jones coworkers all starting singing together to run Glenn out of the breakroom. This time, Glenn went to his supervisor saying, "I'm leaving early today. I've had enough of the foolishness..." "Stop lying Glenn! You're leaving because of this alien thing happening today..." "...I don't care about aliens. I care about peace and quiet. Just like your tone right now is unpleasant. I'm leaving sir, my vacation starts right now." "Where are you going Glenn?"

"Mr. Norman, I'm going home to enjoy my 'Peacecation.' I'll see you in about three months." Glenn stated smiling. Mr. Norman responded, "I can't believe you're using paid sick days and your vacation together. It's actually genius. I'll see you in three months Glenn, unless the aliens destroy us." Mr. Norman laughed as Glenn looked unbothered. Mr. Norman went back into his office as Glenn travelled home.

Glenn stayed in the far suburbs away from the city because he wanted a very quiet environment. It was true what his coworkers said about him winning the lotto. Although Glenn accepted the money anonymously, they still added his name in the newspaper. The same newspaper which happened to be in the company breakroom. No one believed him although he kept denying it. The money all went into a custom built home. Glenn contacted elite sound proofing companies because he desired a fortified sound proofed home. If a nuclear bomb exploded a mile away from his home, he didn't want to hear it. He spent almost all of his winnings sound proofing his home, and he loved it. He didn't have any electronics with bluetooth, no televisions, or radios. His only real device was his smart phone. He had to possess it for his job. The company he worked for had apps employees had to use on certain smart phones and laptops. He didn't want a laptop or a computer. Once he arrived at home, he walked through the first sound proofed door, then he walked through another door which was sound proofed along with the walls. Five feet from this door was another sound proofed door and walls. Once he was inside the interior of his home, he could not hear anything from outside. There were no windows in the interior area of his home. He was a very weird man according to those who knew him. He had a get together one time and his guests were bored to death with nothing to do. No one desired to return. He couldn't keep a woman because he refused to change. His exgirlfriend Ginger, who also loved peace, tried to get Glenn to try counseling or therapy to help with his childhood trauma. He didn't listen to her so she walked away. Nonetheless, he was content. He had to drive a company car which also had company apps installed. If his company needed him, if he was late etc., they could get him as needed. The only sound Glenn enjoyed was the sound of wind blowing when he had the windows down in his car. This was also associated with his childhood. For some reason his parents never fought or argued in the car. They cared about their public reputation. These were Glenn's only good memories. As he drove home, he would lower the windows and smile to himself. This was his favorite part of driving home with little or no traffic. When he arrived to his house, he left the car in the drive way and left his smart phone in the glove compartment. For the next three months he didn't need it. Glenn was very happy to see his groceries were delivered on time. After bringing his groceries into his home, He walked inside smiling because he didn't have to deal with people for three months.

George was feeling better now. Anthony had given him some aspirin to chew just in case he was having a heart attack. He looked a lot better although you could see the concern on his face. The soundwave was ten minutes away from everyone on Earth hearing it, but they could listen to it with their special instruments which were already picking it up. Lisa, being very bold, proclaimed, "I'll listen to it. I'm not afraid to hear what they have to say." No one responded. She walked over to this detailed electronic panel connected to multiple computers. She plugged in the headphones and had a seat. The other four team members gathered around her. "O...k..., here we go." She announced as she reached for the headphones. She placed them on her ears. "I only hear a beep and one word. The word is 'listen.' All I keep hearing is a beep and 'listen' repeatedly."

Lisa turned around to see her teams reaction to what she was hearing. "Where did y'all go? How did y'all walk out of here so quickly?" Lisa started laughing thinking they ran out because they were scared of what she would hear. She removed the headphones and exited the observatory. "Hey!

Where did y'all go so fast?!" Lisa went outside to see if they needed some fresh air. No one was there. She decided to search other areas and could not find her team. She went into the conference room, the break room, and the media room, no one was there. "Where did everyone go?" Lisa talked to herself as she returned to the observatory. Lisa was puzzled as she reentered the observatory. She picked up the phone attempting to call her teammates mobile phones. No one answered. She tried calling colleagues within the building, no one answered. She tried calling her family, no one answered. Dread clutched her emotions. "WHERE IS EVERYONE????!!!!!" She paused. "THIS IS NOT FUNNY!!!!!" Her breathing increased rapidly as her feelings intoxicated her thoughts. Her eyes were looking around the room for her cellphone. She locked on to it and rushed over to grab it. In front of her phone, a lightbulb was bright as the sun it seemed. The Voyager 1 link was connected to their computer. "EVERYONE, VOYAGER 1 IS RECONNECTED!!! COME

SEE THIS!" Lisa screamed. She logged into the computer to check Voyager 1 and observed several data messages which were unread. "How did we miss these?" Lisa uttered thinking how could this be. The computer automatically entered the data into Aitken and the results were presented. Voyager 1 sent a single message saying, "Do not listen." Lisa inhaled all of the oxygen in the world, so it seemed, before she plopped down on a nearby chair as she released an enormous exhale. Her mind was full of questions she said out loud, "How did we miss this message? If it was here the entire time, why didn't we see it? The link was off, how? Where is everyone?... Why did Voyager 1 say, 'Do not listen...?' Wait! OMG!!!..."

"WHERE DID SHE GO?..." "LISA!!!..." "OMG LISA!!!" "SHE DISAPPEARED!!!! WHAT THE FUCK JUST HAPPENED!!!!!???? Raw emotion surfaced from all of the team members as they watched the headphones fall into the empty seat. George apologized for cursing to the team once they all calmed down. "Did the soundwave kill her? Was she vaporized somehow?" Jessica asked with no stumbling in her speech. "We cannot listen to this soundwave. We only have a few minutes before everyone on Earth hears this sound. Frank ran to the landline and made calls informing what just occurred. Frank put the call on speaker. "...Huh? Are you serious Frank? This can't be true." The female voice responded. "I'll patch us into another call already in progress." After connecting the call, the female interrupted the conversation, "...I have extremely valuable information! It needs to be heard now! This is Stephanie with Frank. Frank tell everyone what just happened." Frank wasted no time informing the leaders of nations and the scientific minds of the world what happened to Lisa. No one desired to believe him and multiple arguments took place. It was now down to one minute before everyone could hear the sound. The arguments were so heated, no one bothered to watch the clock as the last ten seconds transpired.

A beep and the word "listen" could be heard all

across the globe. In between the beep was some static no one paid attention to. The conference call was still in progress and everyone listened together. The call didn't drop and no one disappeared. After ten seconds of hearing, someone shouted, "SEE, NO VANISHED FRANK!..." Lisa turned around, "Frank? George? OMG! I THOUGHT Y'ALL WERE GONE FOREVER!!!" The team started celebrating and showing lots of excitement for being reunited with Lisa. "...What's going on? Frank, hello? What is happening?" Stephanie asked hearing the commotion. "Lisa is back! She is back! She says we appeared out of nowhere..." As Frank informed everyone on the phone call, Lisa informed strongly, "VOYAGER 1 LINK IS CONNECTED AND LEFT US A MESSAGE." "I can't hear you both, what did Lisa say Frank?" Stephanie curiously asked. Lisa walked over to the landline phone, "I said Voyager 1 left us a message. Aitken has already examined the data and the message says, 'Do not listen.' However, it's too late for that now." Lisa explained everything to them, and everyone came to the same conclusion. The soundwave caused us to cross over into another dimension. Lisa was alone on the other side until everyone else listened. Lisa walked everyone outside and throughout the facility, everyone from their company was present. They turned on the news and everything looked like our normal world. As they continued talking about the situation, they also realized something important, no one on Earth would have known they crossed over into a parallel universe if it didn't happen to Lisa first. Voyager 1 was the first to cross over, Lisa followed, and now the entire world.

Anthony began saying something which caught the team off guard, but several team members were still talking as he began, "Guys, think about this for a second. Guys, I'm talking. Settle down. Listen to this." Everyone focused as he continued, "Remember when Voyager 1 took pictures of their planet? They were there one second and gone the next, right? This is why they were gone in a second. They crossed over first. Now they have purposely crossed us over with them. Maybe this is going to be an invasion. At some point they will appear in a second. We have to warn the world leaders..." As Anthony shared his findings, the landline phone started ringing. Jessica answered the phone while the team listened to Anthony. Jessica's reaction spoke volumes as the team read her body language. They all stopped talking and approached her together. She placed the headset back on the receiver, "Team, the leaders are aware of everything Anthony just shared with us. Precautions are being heightened." The team looked at each other knowing this could be the end of the world.

The world continued as it did before the soundwave arrived. As the days passed by, the soundwave continued to sound until it was almost unbearable. Everyone across the globe was tortured by this beep and the word listen. On day sixty four, the soundwave was transmitting from every bluetooth device across around the world. Moreover, on this day, the first spaceship instantly became visible over South America. Then Africa, Russia, and the polar caps. This was odd because these ships were over areas and ecosystems with little or no humans. Each ship played the soundwave. While we were trying to understand why these ships were in those areas, more appeared until they covered the entire world and oceans. In unison, each ship began showing a light show of different patterns. These lights also showed on our phones, tablets, computers, laptops, and televisions. Moments later, the people who were deaf started appearing inside nursing homes, hospitals, and other places. They were thought to be missing. We observed many news reports of families and medical facilities saying, "If you have any information of their whereabouts, please contact us immediately." Some families offered rewards. As we witnessed many family reunions, the joy of being reunited ended soon thereafter. Apparently, the aliens appeared showing these light displays on the true Earth to cause the deaf humans to cross over to this dimension. After all the hearing impaired humans were positioned with us, more ships appeared by nursing homes and hospitals. The lights had the same effect as their soundwave. We knew these were the ships that caused the hearing impaired to cross over with us. The sounds playing over ecosystems and oceans brought all of our animal life to this dimension. They made sure the entire Earth was crossed over.

News channels all over the world reported live from most of these ships. Suddenly, a new soundwave was played by each ship and moments later another ship appeared. This ship was bigger and settled over the United Nations. It was like they waited until news crews arrived to speak their announcement. "We told you, if you respond, we would come. This is now our planet. Every living thing on this planet will be our food; including you. When you rise up to defend yourselves, we will show you our might. As you humans say, 'We dare you.' We dare you to attack us. After you make your feeble attempt, we will eat you alive. Your animals will be food for our animals. There is no place for any of you to hide. Your underground bunkers will hold you like your refrigerators for us to open and eat at our leisure. Even if you decide to commit suicide, we will bring you back to life and dine on you until your heart gives out. You will be eaten alive just like the other worlds. Just like them, you sent a probe to show us how to find you. Thank you. Our whole civilization will dine on your whole civilization. I look forward to all five of my mouths chewing on your flesh. Prepare to be our meals humans."

This transmission was spoken in every language across our planet. Each nation mobilized their military against their spaceships. Every missle, and all artillery fired, became stationary in the air. Our fighter planes suddenly stopped mid-flight as they maneuvered and the pilots couldn't eject. Our fighter planes slowly floated to the alien ships as we all watched on the news. The planes were landed on the platform of their ships. A very wide access door opened. The world saw the aliens as they slowly walked out moving like herds of Wildebeest toward the planes. They had five enormous strong muscular legs, big wide long bony feet, and a huge body like a hippo. Their head was on the top middle section of their jet black slimy body with five glowing yellow tiny eyes in a circle. They had two massive long strong arms with wide hand type appendages with ten grasping fingerlike appendages. The people who were present and witnessed the alien race screamed at their appearance, and started running or driving away. The aliens approached the planes in dramatic fashion. They easily ripped open the planes until the pilots were exposed. Each alien picked up a pilot and raised them up high over their head. They knew the entire world was watching as their representative announced, "Humans, it's dinner time!" Then released a very dark evil laugh. "Do you love my laughter? I saw it in your horror movies." Then they all shared evil laughter together. The pilots were yelling in fear knowing they were about to be eaten alive. Although it appeared they didn't have any mouths, their anatomy transformed. Their head lifted up slowly revealing a thick wide neck. We now saw five openings that had extensions moving out. These five protruding objects looked like arms waving freely until the very end of each retracted. They appeared to be four feet in length. Circular mouths six inches in diameter with very sharp looking teeth moved slowly toward each of the pilots individually. I wanted to look away, but I was paralyzed with fright. The aliens tore into the pilots. You could hear each of them scream as they were eaten alive. News networks tried to stop the live broadcast, but the alien technology was in control. They made us watch. You couldn't turn off your television, laptop, computer, or smartphone. All devices remained on even if the battery died. In many cities people ran away from the ships, but like the fighter planes, they stopped them from running. Aliens leaped from their ships to the ground dining on the humans who were immobilized. Tanks, and other military vehicles, couldn't move after arriving to aid the fighter pilots. The aliens ripped open the tanks with their brute strength. Seeing our military eaten alive was disheartening. Our bravest and best were defensiveless as they were devoured. Each of the five mouths bit chunks out causing blood to spray everywhere. They gorged on our soldiers. The parts they didn't eat remained.

In areas where there were no spaceships, humanity hid themselves. We couldn't be out in the open. We were hopeless. There was no mercy. In the major cities, skyscrapers were destroyed to reveal the humans hiding inside. Although the building fell to the ground, the people inside didn't die. It's like the aliens injected us all with a preservative until they dined on us alive. It was unbelievable. We knew this was our end. Some of us tried to commit suicide, but the wounds would heal. Something in those soundwaves changed us. We truly became their food. The Earth was now their buffet and every living thing was on the menu.

After only seventy five days, humanity and animal life was on the brink of extinction. We were herded and floated up to their ships. Many of us grieved for humanity. We began to despise science knowing it led us to our own demise. We were some of the last remaining humans. We didn't have to worry about food or drink. What the aliens did to us genuinely made us food for them. We weren't hungry or thirsty. If we died they brought us back to life. Our spirit was obliterated. There was no more fight in us. Every time we made an effort of any kind, we were paused, stopped in our tracks, and eventually eaten alive. Adults, children, babies, old, young, skinny, fat, and obese, were all feasted on alive. Every weapon we fired is still motionless in the air. Then it finally happened. An alien ship came to our location. We were hoping something from Voyager 1 could help us fight back. We were all searching for a miracle, but that never happened. They destroyed the roof off our facility in search of their next meal. Once our coworkers were found, they were stopped as we ran. The aliens continued searching for more of us through every building until they finally arrived at our observatory. They used their weapon to blow up our observatory. Although we were covered in debris, we didn't die. I didn't feel pain of any kind for some reason. The entire facility was destroyed just like the White House. We watched the aliens as they floated the rubble from the White House away from where it originally stood. Then a different kind of light shined from their ship straight down where the White House used to stand. The ground shook vehemently as it opened up. Everything under the White House began to rise up until the underground bunker with the President was now on the surface. It hovered there for a minute in theatrical style. Suddenly it dropped on the front lawn splitting in half. The President stood still as his Secret Service men ran trying to evade. Just like all other humans, they became stationary. A single alien leaped from their ship and stood in front of the President. This was the alien representative. "The leader of the free world will be my personal delicacy. I'm the leader of our world which is truly free. Would you like to address the world Mr. President?" The President of the United States was allowed to move freely and speak, "Humanity, I would like to apologize to you. When we launched Voyager 1 and 2, we never dreamed we would bring a threat to our very existence. Say your prayers. Love each other. Forgive each other. I'll see you all in heaven." The President faced the alien which towered over him by two feet and asked, "What is your name?" "I was not expecting this question. No other race across the universe has ever asked my name. My name is DIN. Pleased to eat you." The alien laughed in the Presidents face. "I personally eat all world leaders. Rest in peace as you say on this planet." DIN uttered as he signaled more aliens to leap from the ship. They stood in front of the secret service. The President was eaten by DIN. The other aliens jumped up and down as DIN savored the President alive. DIN declared with his one mouth not eating the President, "You did not try to run. You do not scream in agony. You are a respectable meal. I salute you. I respect you." For a second the President looked grateful for the compliment as the fifth mouth joined the four other mouths gnashing into his body. DIN released his mouths from the remains of the President and looked at the aliens with him and shouted to them, **"DINE ON THEM!!!"** Unlike the President, they yelled and screamed in terror. So much so, they died with horror frozen in the faces.

What the aliens did was a show of their strength and the superiority of their technology. They demonstrated we couldn't protect our leaders. This was to break the fight in us globally; and it did, it actually did. The Air Force and Navy sent more fighter jets to no avail. The missles were motionless like the others. The one thing I noticed this time was the fact that the missles followed the ships. They must have a shield that holds our weapons in a permanent stationary position. I suppose this was to remind us not to even try to defeat them.

Well, like I was saying, our observatory was destroyed just like the White House. When we were floated up to their platform, we didn't get a speech. Without hesitation we were all eaten alive.

This is when I felt pain. Their razor sharp teeth tore into my body easily. I could hear my bones shatter. I heard them as they crunched and chewed on me. I still couldn't move, but I could see. My sight was limited to the direction I faced. I witnessed George and Jessica being eaten alive. The aliens loved our screams of pain. It was as if it made us taste even better. Anthony and Lisa were behind me, but I could hear their agonizing yells. Our team was eaten alive together. The parts of us they didn't eat, they tossed back down to what was left of our observatory. After hitting the ground, what remained of my body died almost instantly. My consciousness faded into darkness and I despised science.

A week later, there were no more humans or animal life on Earth. Everyone hiding underground were found, just like the President, and other world leaders. Submarines were surfaced from deep in the oceans, and they dined on those soldiers. Their ships were big enough to pack us up like groceries for the journey back to their planet. They weren't interested in habitating the Earth. Our major cities were left in ruins. They destroyed every structure looking for us and made sure no humans were left behind.

As they were in the process of transforming their ships, and everyone aboard, into soundwaves to return to their planet, Glenn exited his home early on a Monday morning. Everything looked normal to him. He had no knowledge the Earth was invaded and didn't know what happened to humanity. Although his home was destroyed on the parallel side, there was nothing wrong with his home. As a matter of fact, as he exited his home, the destruction of his home was reversed on the other side. Glenn was smiling and happy he didn't have to hear anything from anyone during his peacecation. He went awol for another week more, because he didn't desire to go back to work. Glenn had enough money saved if his job decided to fire him, but he honestly didn't care. He looked around his lawn causing his smile to fade fast. His landscaping was not tended to as usual. He paid a local landscaping company every two weeks and thought to himself, "Why didn't they come? Maybe there is an issue with my bank account." He walked to his car (which was destroyed on the other side, also repaired itself like his home), started the engine, lowered the windows, grabbed his phone, and turned it on. As he sat in his car, everything on the other side mirrored his side. For some reason, everything eyed in Glenn's world caused a response on the parallel side. A response which restored all the destruction caused by the aliens. After turning on his phone, and seeing the battery fully charged, he logged into his bank account. He noticed there were no deductions. He located the lawn service on his bill pay link and paid them immediately.

As Glenn began his drive to the city, the streets and highways had vehicles cluttered. On the parallel side, everything repaired itself and mirrored what Glenn eyed. He drove passed many vehicles and noticed they were all empty. He stopped and wondered why empty vehicles were on the roads. Some blocked him entirely making him drive around these vehicles on the grass. This was very odd to Glenn. He was perplexed trying to figure out why cars were on the wrong side going away from the city, facing him, in the wrong direction. As he got closer to the city, he couldn't navigate the highway anymore because cars completely blocked him. He turned around and went back to the last exit thinking why the cars were empty. Then he thought, "I haven't seen one person. Where is everyone? Is this because of the soundwave?"

Glenn decided to stop at his favorite coffee shop since he hasn't enjoyed his choice of delicious brew in three months or so. As he made his way to the coffee shop, he immediately noticed he didn't see anyone walking or driving. He drove by a dog park and there were no dogs or dog owners present. Screeetchhhhhh!!!!!! He abruptly stopped his car! He exited his car to look around. Although he loved the silence, he actually enjoyed watching dogs playing with other dogs. He decided to call his job, just to see if anyone would answer. Glenn called every department and no one answered. "What is going on here?" Glenn said to himself wondering what happened while he was on his peacecation. He jumped into his car and drove to the coffee shop only a few blocks away. He logged into his app and ordered his favorites because he hated lines. This was done out of habit although he hasn't seen anyone. Glenn waited a few minutes and walked into the coffee shop with his order already paid for. When he approached the app checkout line, his order was waiting for him although he didn't see any employees. No one was in line and no one was on their laptops working. "Hello!?" Glenn looked around and shouted again, "Hello!?" No one responded. "Who made my order? Can you come out please?" No one joined him and no one answered. He checked his order and it was exactly correct. He tasted his coffee and it was perfect; hot and perfect. He gathered his order and exited the coffee shop confused with everything.

Glenn walked around looking at everything and

seeing no one. No one could be seen in any direction. The silence was welcomed to a certain extent, but Glenn never dreamed the silence in the world would be equivalent to the silence inside his home. There was not even a sound of birds singing. No freight trains. No airplanes. No city workers or contruction workers. The only thing which looked normal were the unoccupied vehicles mimicing rush hour traffic. He finally walked to his car and headed to work. As he approached downtown, the streets were filled with empty cars. He had to park his car and walk sixteen blocks to work.

As Glenn walked to work, everything on the other side rebuilt itself. The remains of the dead which the aliens left, began to regain their flesh and were soon alive again. They didn't understand why or how they came back to life, but remembered everything that occurred to cause their death. A nearby alien ship witnessed the buildings being restored and was astonished how this could be happening. No other world they conquered, with their soundwave weapons. had this happen.

Another thing which transpired, shocking the aliens, was the fact they began to vomit the remains of the humans they had eaten. Every human in the surrounding downtown area, eaten by aliens, was restored to their body in the place they were exactly when the aliens arrived. This only happened in the areas where Glenn visited. However things were supposed to be in Glenn's world was reflected on the other side. For some reason, Glenn's reality dominated both. He was clueless of this, but as he walked to work, downtown, and the lives of those lost, were being reinstated exactly how it was before the soundwave arrived. The aliens reported this to DIN. He was trying to understand what was happening to put a stop to it. The alien scientists went to work trying to find the reason and solution to what was happening.

The aliens tried to use their technology once again, but this time it didn't work. No humans were floated up to their ships and the humans could move freely. One alien ship was above the building where Glenn worked. As Glenn approached his building, all the weapons which were fired at the alien ships, those that were stopped in the air, activated and hit the alien ships. The aliens didn't know what happened or why it happened. Glenn took the elevator up to his floor and found no one. He looked around the entire floor and actually missed his coworkers. The silence seemed to stress him as he couldn't find one human in the city.

Glenn sat as his console and began to make phone calls to his family, former friends, and business networks. No one answered, however, Glenn calling them began to reinstate them, and all animals of the world connected to those areas included. Everyone connected through the mobile phone companies, and the cell tower providers were restored. In the areas where these people were located, the weapons paused the by alien ships began activating and hitting the ships. Glenn's determination to find life on Earth helped save our planet. When he logged into the internet, everyone and everything linked to his internet connection was restored. He called all branches of the military and soldiers who were eaten came back to life. All of the tanks, fighter planes, submarines, etc., were restored and the military attacked the alien ships who's technology no longer worked. As the military leaders contacted other militaries across the globe, those soldiers, leaders, buildings, weapons, etc., were reinstated as well. Until finally, Glenn called his brother at the observatory. We all came back to life and didn't know why, but we worked to find out. As we called other agencies, they were restored and after eight hours, it seemed the entire world was back to normal.

There was one alien ship which remained in space which orbited our planet. The damaged alien ships couldn't leave our atmosphere, so the last ship entered our planet trying to help the other ships. A very loud soundwave was emitted with bright flashing lights, and all humanity feared. This was the aliens last chance and last resort. Although it appeared we could win this thing, we weren't sure what was to become of this new soundwave.

This new soundwave penatrated both sides of

the parallel universe. However, Glenn was already back home being that it was more than eight hours later. While he was at work, he did his job which also helped restore and reinstate those via the internet connected with his work. The next day Glenn didn't bother leaving his home. He believed everyone was gone and he was the only one left. He was pleased when he returned home seeing his landscaping was completed. He called them to thank them for their work, but no one answered. Glenn soon realized every desire of his was granted although no one was present to perform the task he desired; such as what he ordered on the coffee app. Earlier this night, on his way home from work, he stopped at a fast food drive-thru. No one said anything, but he ordered just to see if his order would be completed. When he arrived at the window, his order was waiting for him. Glenn was speechless, but happy. Once he was home, he enjoyed his meal in the silence he loved so much. He never heard the new soundwave which came hours later that night.

As the new soundwave continued to play, nothing happened to us. We could still move freely and the militaries across the globe began to attack this ship. It's like the aliens had no defense. This time our weapons freely hit the ship. No more pausing. There were no counterattacks of any kind. It's like the aliens didn't have soldiers of their own. We kept attacking repeatedly. Our manufacturers were making more missles and weapons to stock pile reserves. We wanted to make sure no one ran out of weapons. Smaller nations had help from larger nations. Enemy nations helped each other. All of humanity came together as one. There was a 24 hour attack on these alien ships which did not stop.

At our observatory, we had several ideas we could not explain scientifically. George believed his brother was the reason for our reinstatement. He believed his brother's reality superceded our parallel world. Nothing made logical sense, but this seemed to make sense to us. As all of us came together and shared our philosophies with our colleagues, we called it, "The Law Of First." Our theory was our true existence overpowered the false existence. Although this world looked exactly like our true world, it wasn't true and therefore, the things which are taking place in our true existence were being established in this false world. As long as someone dwells in our real world, we had a chance to defeat these aliens in this false world. Of course, this brings us to this other conclusion: if Glenn dies we lose.

Fortunately for us, the new soundwave started having a lower frequency. At first we believed they were trying to do something different, but as the soundwave continued to get lower, we understood the aliens were losing their powersource. They packed us up quickly and were ready to leave, but the unthinkable happened for them. As our militaries attacked their ships, they tried to turn all of their ships into soundwaves. We saw them as if they were turning translucent, but our militaries bombarded them with all out missle assaults. All fighter planes, tanks, naval ships, and submarines all fleed from the alien ships. We didn't know what our world leaders were doing. They sent bombers to hit each alien ship with an Eletromagnetic Pulse (EMP). Each alien ship was immediately disabled and started free falling down. Those who were in the vacinity of these ships ran to avoid being crushed. Everyone scattered!!! Each of these ships were about three miles in length and width. Some people knew it was too late to run. They stood there looking up with courage knowing at least we have beaten these aliens. Some people were even high-fiving each other as they ships were about to crush them. As they looked up at the ships coming down upon them, they disappearred. Every ship disappearred before our eyes. We didn't know what happened, but we celebrated. Maybe the aliens turned into soundwaves and went back to their planet. We didn't know, but we were happy.

Suddenly, George had an idea. He gathered us all together and we took the observatory helicopter. He didn't bother explaining as we took off. He instructed the operator and took a seat with us.

"Team, I believe we are now back in our real world. We are on our way to my brother's house. If I'm correct, he's inside his home. If not, we are still in this parallel world. I'm not calling him because he probably won't answer. I have to see if he's home." It took about forty minutes to land at Glenn's home. He didn't have a door bell and knocking on his door wasn't working. We waited outside his home about an hour when George decided we should leave, and get back to work at the observatory. As our helicoper took off, Glenn exited his home. Our pilot shouted, "IS THAT YOUR BROTHER!?" "OH MY GOSH YES! LAND! PLEASE LAND!" George ran to his brother Glenn. Glenn looked relieved to see his brother. They happily embraced. After a few words, which we couldn't hear, they both boarded the helicoper and we went back to the observatory.

Everything was explained to Glenn and Glenn shared his experience. All of the pieces were put together and shared with the world leaders. We all came to the same conclusion. The aliens power source was depleted which placed us back in our original state. We didn't know if the aliens returned to their planet, or if they were stuck on the parallel Earth, but we were satisfied we weren't extinct. Glenn was celebrated and acknowledged as a hero to our planet, and was rewarded tremendously. Mankind established world-wide treaties and the global economy thrived with everyone working together so we all could prosper in our present world.